MUSIC HALL QUEEN

Anna Markland

OLIVERHEBERBOOKS

Dedicated to Dame Gracie Fields, our 'Lancashire Lass.'

Chapter 1

Sing, Oh Sing

Bolton, Lancashire, England, 1862

Fortified by a last gulp of gin straight from the bottle, Maggie left her untidy dressing room and strolled along the dimly-lit corridor. Faded portraits of past stars nailed to the dingy walls whispered encouragement. Stagehands and other members of the show's cast bustled about, dodging racks laden with costumes that had seen better days. The air was filled with nervous excitement, despite the fact the same show went on night after night.

Pausing in the darkened wings, Maggie took a deep breath before stepping onto the polished wooden floor of the stage. When the once-luxurious red velvet curtains rose like an inverted waterfall, the deafening applause lifted her spirits. The rowdy, clog-stomping crowd up in the gallery loved her, whistling and hooting when she thrust out her breasts and slowly lifted the hem of her gown to reveal a shapely calf. Disappointed groans greeted the moment she coquettishly lowered the hem to conceal her leg once more.

The cheering resumed when the small orchestra in the pit struck up the familiar introduction to her opening number.

Twirling the handle of the silk parasol nestled on her shoulder, she launched into the lyrics, confident the high, vaulted ceiling would capture and enhance the sound of her voice. Every note, every word would reach the farthest corners. Her song would fill the space and envelop the audience in the magic.

> *In the heart of Lancashire, where the looms hum*
> *loud,*
> *The mill towns rise, bustling and proud.*
> *From dawn till dusk, we weave and spin,*
> *But when the sun sets, let the music begin.*

The orchestra's volume increased, but the appreciative audience couldn't wait to join in the chorus and drown out the musicians when she encouraged them to sing along with her.

> *Sing, oh sing, the songs of the music hall,*
> *With laughter and joy, we'll answer the call.*
> *From the rhythm of work to the beat of the night,*
> *In our Lancashire hearts, we find pure delight.*

Strutting across the stage, she began the second verse:

> *So let's raise a glass to the nights filled with*
> *cheer...*

She paused, knowing this suggestion would be greeted with the usual raised glasses and toasts.

> *To the songs that remind us of all we hold dear.*
> *With each note we sing, we honor our past,*
> *In the legacy of laughter, our bonds will hold*
> *fast.*

The audience belted out the chorus again. *"Sing, oh sing…"*

WHEN THE SONG WAS OVER, she took her bow, acknowledging the applause by placing both hands over her heart. She was proud to be part of an institution that had provided fun and laughter for generations. She could almost hear the applause of countless audiences past. Every step on the creaky wooden floor echoed with memories of shows gone by. The soft glow of the gas floodlights made it almost impossible to see her audience or the tawdry frescoes of the once opulent *Hippodrome Music Hall*. Nor could she see her husband, but she knew Fred was out there, watching, waiting, deciding whether he would beat her for flirting too much with the punters or not enough.

However, she couldn't afford to think about the misery of life with Fred as she launched into the comedy part of her routine. There'd be time enough to drown her sorrows after the performance.

"I went to Blackpool on holiday and knocked at the first boarding house I came to," she began, not surprised when a hush fell. The audience hadn't heard this one before and she doubted it would go over well. Taking a deep breath, she carried on. "A woman stuck her head out of an upstairs window and said, 'What do you want?' I said, 'I'd like to stay here'. She said, 'Ok. Stay there'."

The audience groaned loud enough to drown out the drummer's *ba dum tss*. As she'd expected, this new joke was a flop. Fred would punish her for it, though he'd thought it hilarious and insisted she include it in her repertoire. Hoping to restore the happy mood, she resorted to an old favorite. "I went to see a friend who works in a cotton mill," she began. "He wasn't there. He had gone for cotton."

"Gone for cotton," came the jubilant echo.

"Went back a week later, same thing. Gone for cotton."

"Gone for cotton," the punters shouted gleefully.

"A week later I was told he had died, so I went to the cemetery. On his headstone it said...."

"Gone but not for cotton," the audience yelled.

They'd heard the joke a thousand times but it still resonated. The drummer played four rim shots. The audience repeated the punch line over and over as they laughed and cheered, most of them three sheets to the wind. She didn't care. The common people loved her and she was safe with them.

She followed up with another favorite. "What do you call a mill that's just okay?"

"A satisfactory," came the raucous reply as the drummer's rim shot teased once more.

Blowing kisses to the audience, she left the stage to wait in the wings until her next appearance.

Cheers resounded as the popular monologist appeared on stage. Declaiming amusing monologues was a long-standing tradition in Lancashire. Maggie always enjoyed Ernest Holloway's performance, and the audience never knew which poem he might declaim. They applauded loudly when he embarked on the *Tale of Timmy and the Bear*.

> *There's a tale from the zoo, quite a story,*
> *About young Timmy and the bear's territory.*
> *A lad with a grin, not a worry or care,*
> *He ventured too close to the big grizzly bear.*

"Oooh," the audience yelled.

> *Now Timmy was known for his curious ways,*
> *Exploring the world on those warm summer*
> *days.*

He'd seen every creature, from zebras to deer,
But the bear was the one that he held most dear.
With his family in tow, they arrived at the cage,
Timmy's eyes widened with excitement, not rage.
Ignoring the signs that were plain to be read,
He edged near the bars with bravery instead.

"Oh-oh," everyone shouted.

The bear in the corner, lounging with grace,
Lifted its head and gave Timmy a face.
With a yawn and a stretch, it ambled to see,
What this young lad might be bringing for tea.
Now Timmy, not fazed by the bear's advance,
Giggled and waved, as if in a trance.
His parents were shouting, "Step back, my dear!"
But Timmy just smiled, feeling no fear.

"Step back, Timmy," the crowd urged.

The bear gave a growl, not menacing, just mild,
A warning to Timmy, who was still just a child.
With a start, Timmy stepped back, a lesson he
    learned,
A boundary respected, and respect he earned.
The family breathed easy, crisis averted,
And Timmy's adventure was joyfully diverted.
So next time you're tempted to venture too near,
Remember young Timmy and the bear that was
    dear.

Laughter and applause rang out as Ernest left the stage, to be followed by the tap dancer.

The audience clapped along with the dancer's impressive footwork. Maggie tapped her feet. At the end of his performance, she filled her lungs and prepared for her second appearance.

~

"Hurry, we'll be late," Edouard urged as he watched the manager of his store fumble with the keys to the heavy plate glass front door of *Shangri-La*.

"You go ahead," Foster replied. "I'll lock up, though it's a mystery to me why you're in such a hurry. There'll be other acts."

"But you know very well Miss Maggie is the best performer at *The Hippodrome*," he explained. "She's talented and beautiful."

"True," Foster allowed. "But you're Edouard Deschanel, the French owner of the biggest and best new department store in Bolton, the *Shangri-La*. You should be keeping up appearances by patronizing *The Theatre Royal*. More upper class."

Edouard chuckled. "You forgot to mention the *Shangri-La* is the **only** high-class department store in town."

"Hence its popularity with the who's who of Bolton," Foster quipped as the stubborn lock finally clicked into place. "And other parts of Lancashire."

"Come on," Edouard replied. "We might still be in time."

Breathless after dodging the crowds on Deansgate, they passed the market cross, commemorated with a brass plaque as the execution place of the Earl of Derby two centuries before, during the Civil War, and finally strode into the ornate entryway of *The Hippodrome* in Churchgate.

Edouard inhaled deeply. The air in the old theater was always thick with the scent of history. The intricate woodwork and time-worn carved statues in the entrance spoke of bygone elegance. It was akin to entering a realm of grandeur and gaiety. Gas lamps cast a welcoming glow. The foyer buzzed with anticipation. "Don't you find this place invigorating?" he asked Foster.

"I suppose so. It provides people with an escape from the monotony of daily life."

"Has Miss Maggie been on yet?" Edouard asked the man in the booth, handing over the sixpence entry fee.

"Tha's the French fella from that there new fancy store on Deansgate," came the reply.

"*Oui*, the *Shangri-La*," Edouard replied with a smile. He was impatient to end the conversation but business always came first. "Have you paid us a visit?"

"Took the missus there, but it's a bit pricey fer the likes o' us. 'Ere's tha tickets."

He offered his thanks and gave the tickets to the usher who promptly tore them in two.

THE AUDIENCE CHEERED LOUDLY when the orchestra played the opening bars of Maggie's final song.

A hush fell when she intoned the introductory words to the plaintive strains of a solitary violin.

> *What's the use o' fashin', lads, this life's nay so*
> > *long,*
> *So, if you gather round, I'll try my hand at a*
> > *song.*
> *It may show a guidin' glimmer to some wand'rer*
> > *astray,*
> *Or, haply, gi' some poor owd soul a lift on*
> > *the way.*

Swaying to the music, the audience solemnly echoed the refrain as the whole orchestra played. *A lift on the way, a lift on the way.*

> *Oh, there's some folk who walk, an' there's some*
> *who ride,*
> *But, never mortal man can tell what chance may*
> *betide.*
> *To-day, he may be blossomin', like roses in May.*
> *Soon, he may be beggin' for a lift on the way.*

The audience's voices filled the hall. *A lift on the way, a lift on the way. He may soon be beggin' for a lift on the way.*

Maggie inhaled deeply, ready to sing the verse she loved the most. It spoke of the generosity for which the working folk of Lancashire were famous.

> *Goodwill, it's a jewel, where there's little else to*
> *spare;*
> *An' a man may help another though his purse*
> *may be bare;*
> *A gen'rous heart, like sunshine, brings good*
> *cheer in its ray,*
> *An' a friendly word can sometimes give a lift on*
> *the way.*

A hundred voices echoed the refrain. *A lift on the way, a lift on the way,*
An' a friendly word can sometimes give a lift on the way.
Together, Maggie and her audience belted out the last line. *Pray heaven may give us all a lift on the way.*

. . .

As Maggie blew a kiss and took her bow, she was acutely aware of the legacy of which she was part. *The Hippodrome* had been a haven for artists and audiences for decades, a place where dreams came true, if only in one's imagination. Notwithstanding the misery of her own life with Fred, she took comfort in the knowledge she was adding her talent to the rich tapestry of performances that had graced the historic theater.

The arrival on stage of the can-can dancers only added to the joyous uproar.

~

Shown to their table, Edouard was disappointed to see Miss Maggie blow a kiss to her appreciative audience and leave the stage as the can-can dancers came on.

He'd missed her performance, but she always came into the hall to mingle with the patrons. If she stopped by his table, he'd seize the opportunity to introduce himself to a woman he felt inextricably drawn to.

He took a moment to gaze about. The old theater had seen better days, but traces of its bygone opulence lingered. Intricate crystal chandeliers hung from the high vaulted ceiling. The air was filled with the aroma of ladies' perfumes, tobacco and roasted chestnuts bought from outside street vendors.

Boisterous working class patrons contributed to the lively atmosphere. Somehow, the music hall managed to banish the divide between the wealthy patrons sitting at tables in the main hall and the working poor in the gallery.

Chapter 2

Attraction

Occasionally waving to the boisterous crowd in the gallery, Maggie wandered from table to table, exchanging pleasantries with the patrons able to afford the slightly more expensive seats on the main floor of the music hall.

She tried hard to keep the smile plastered on her face, but Fred's scowling presence in the shadows under the gallery at the back of the hall weighed on her heart. She licked her lips, wishing she could tipple a quick tumbler of gin.

She recognized most of the regular patrons and steered clear of the men who deemed it their God-given right to smack her bottom or fondle her breasts. After all, she was just a music hall floozy.

She startled when one handsome patron stood, took her hand and bestowed a courtly kiss on her knuckles.

"Edouard Deschanel at your service, lovely lady," he crooned. "Proprietor of *Shangri-La.* Dare I hope you'll favor us with your patronage?"

She'd seen him watching her on previous evenings but this was the first time he'd spoken to her. It was nothing more than an attempt on the punter's part to promote his business, but

Fred wouldn't see it that way. All he'd see was the fierce blush reddening her face, and he'd know the gentlemanly gesture and the intriguing foreign accent had affected her. He saw naught amiss with drunken mill owners like Roderick Hampson sliding their hands up her skirts, but wouldn't understand gentlemanly behavior. She withdrew her hand quickly, hoping to calm her racing heart before she had to face her husband's anger. Fred was no gentleman. He believed it his right to flirt with other women, but if Maggie so much as looked at another man …

Fred would recognize a lie if she claimed the admiration in the shopkeeper's dark eyes hadn't flooded her body with wanton feelings she'd long since thought dead and buried. Hoping to avoid her husband, she headed for her dressing room and the hidden gin bottle.

"CAN we get some service 'ere or art too busy oglin' Miss Maggie?"

Emerson Dean startled, gooseflesh marching up his spine. If the customers had noticed their waiter's fawning attention to Maggie, Fred Chadwick might have seen his fascination too, and Fred was a jealous man who was always handy with his fists. It was ironic—Fred was brazen in his liaisons with other women and bragged of beating his wife, whereas Emerson worshipped the ground Maggie walked on and would never treat her so cruelly.

He snarled at the French chap who'd kissed Maggie's hand. Emerson had seen him watching Maggie with rapt attention for a few days now. Fred wouldn't take too kindly to that, especially since the customer's actions had made her blush. Or perhaps he'd said something risqué. He was French after all.

"Sorry, gents," he replied, as he turned away from the stage, his heart sinking when he recognized a group of wealthy regulars—mill owners who always tipped well. "You must agree Miss Maggie is captivating," he sighed, assuming his best smile.

"Aye," they agreed. "Fetch us another pitcher of ale."

Emerson had a difficult time understanding how these men managed to afford several nights out every week when their mills sat idle because of the cotton famine brought about by the American Civil War. However, it was his job to wait on them, not speculate on their finances. "Right away," he replied, casting an anxious glance about to make sure Fred Chadwick wasn't watching him from the shadows at the back of the hall. He needn't have worried. Fred was too busy glaring at the Frenchman.

"He's following her to the dressing room," he told Foster, nodding at the scowling brute who'd emerged from the shadows at the back of the hall. "Just like last night."

Foster frowned. "That's Fred Chadwick," he replied. "Her husband."

The news knotted Edouard's innards. He'd fully intended to pursue Miss Maggie. She ignited desires he'd thought dead and buried after the untimely death of his French wife. "I don't like the look of him," he said.

"That's all well and good, but it's common knowledge he's not a man to mess with," his manager cautioned.

Laced with a hint of fear, the words of warning were enough to confirm Edouard's suspicion that Miss Maggie was married to an abusive husband. He abhorred men who victimized women. "We'll see about that," he said.

FRED CHADWICK SEETHED. First of all, Maggie had crucified the new joke he'd instructed her to tell, then she'd flirted with the Frenchman who'd recently become a regular. As if that weren't enough to rouse a man's justifiable ire, the milksop who waited tables had ogled Maggie in his usual gawping fashion. He'd have a word with Emerson Dean, although it probably wasn't worth his time and effort. The man wore so much perfumed pomade in his hair, even Maggie wouldn't be interested.

Fists clenched, he decided to deal with his wife before he did anything else.

Chapter 3

Confrontation

Satisfied a painful arm twisting and a few jabs in the ribs had made it crystal clear to his sobbing wife he didn't appreciate her flirting with the punters, Fred Chadwick left Maggie's dressing room. He took the last swig of the gin she thought she could hide from him and threw the empty green bottle against the wall. "Stupid bitch," he cursed.

The foreign chap who'd kissed his wife's hand was still sitting at his table. The Frog glared at him as if he were the guilty party. Fred should waylay him on his way out and let him know proprietorship of a fancy department store on Deansgate didn't entitle him to flirt with Maggie.

However, that would have to wait. He had more pleasurable pursuits to take care of. The new cigarette girl had rebuffed his initial advances, but she was just being shy. Sooner or later, she'd fall for his flattery—they always did, else they'd be unemployed.

With most millworkers out of work thanks to the cotton famine, jobs were hard to come by. Maria was her family's only wage earner. Before the week was out, she'd be his latest conquest. His rod hardened just thinking about her struggles to fight him off.

He espied Maria heading for a group of patrons in the rear of the hall, the tray she carried full of Carreras cigars and cigarettes. Once she'd waited on them, he'd draw her into the shadows and get his hands on her tempting little titties.

Edouard feigned interest in the comedian telling corny jokes but he seethed inwardly when Fred Chadwick reappeared from the corridor. Adjusting the cuffs of his sleeves, Chadwick had the smug air of a man full of his own superiority. He'd often seen that look on the face of his abusive father. "I'll wager he's beaten Miss Maggie," he told Foster.

"Let it go," Foster replied. "It's none of our business."

"I'm going to make it my business," Edouard retorted, narrowing his eyes at Chadwick who was now stalking the cigarette girl. "He's a *prédateur*, a predator."

"Again, stay out of it," Foster advised.

Edouard had stayed out of his parents' violent relationship and eventually his father had beaten his mother to death. "I can't," he replied, torn between checking on Maggie and coming to the rescue of the cigarette girl.

Maggie won out. He left the table and negotiated the cluttered corridor in search of her dressing room.

"Go away," Maggie rasped when someone tapped lightly at the door of her dressing room.

"It's Edouard Deschanel, Mrs. Chadwick. Are you all right?"

The French accent washed over her. She'd been instantly attracted to the handsome stranger when he'd kissed her hand, but he mustn't see her trembling with fear and hopeless rage. "I'm fine," she lied, cradling her sore ribs.

"I don't believe you," came the reply. "May I enter?"

It was foolhardy, but she gripped the side of her dressing table and stood with difficulty. Pain arrowed into her abdomen but she couldn't let him think she was a cowed and broken woman. Nor could she allow him close enough to smell the gin on her breath.

"*Entray, monsewer,*" she said, fanning her mouth and wondering where she found the courage to flirt with this overly attractive man. If Fred ever got wind of the Frenchman's presence in her dressing room ...

When he entered, the concern in his dark eyes broke her heart. Why couldn't she have married a compassionate man like this stranger? But she knew the answer. Swept off her feet by Fred's charm, she'd gullibly made excuses for his more disturbing traits.

"Sit, if you please, Madame," he said, hurrying to help her regain her seat. "Your husband has struck you, yes?"

"He didn't mean to," she lied, glad to sit down slowly with his help. "It was my fault."

"You don't really believe that, do you? I know his type. He doesn't need an excuse to beat you."

Maggie couldn't summon the energy to argue. "If he finds you here, he'll do more than beat me."

"I won't allow it."

For a fleeting moment, Maggie thought she'd found a champion, but that was wishful thinking. Gin was her solace. "He's my husband. He has the right to beat me."

He shook his head. "You're not strong enough to challenge him, but I am. Bullies are cowards."

"I can't ask that of you."

"You don't have to ask," he replied, coming close enough for her to smell his subtle cologne. "I will gladly defend your honor."

There was something about this man that drew her. The temptation to stand and throw herself into his arms was powerful. He lowered his head, his tempting lips so close. But she was afraid. He must be able to smell the gin. "Fred might come back any moment."

"No, he won't. He's busy chasing after the cigarette girl."

The knot in her belly tightened as she struggled to her feet. For Fred to abuse his wife was one thing, but Maria was an innocent. "He might be sorry. Maria has a jealous boyfriend, the theater's strongman."

He shrugged as he took her hands and drew her gently into his arms. "I am drawn to you, Maggie," he whispered. "Let me take care of you."

"You can't," she replied, gritting her teeth against the pain when she reluctantly pulled away. "I'm married."

"Very well. I will leave you to recover. But I'm a persistent man."

He bestowed a kiss on the back of her hand and left, but there was no mistaking the determination in his dark eyes.

At the back of the hall, Fred stood so close to Maria, he could smell her cheap scent. Once he had her in his bed, he'd buy her something better. A man had a right to fill his nostrils with expensive perfume while he fucked a woman.

When she moved away from the punters she was serving, he squeezed her bottom. Startled, she whirled around, nigh on hitting him with the tray she carried. She narrowed her eyes when she saw who had touched her so intimately. Satisfied she feared him, he bent his head, intending to steal a kiss. Without warning, Goliath loomed out of the shadows behind Maria. She moved toward the show's strongman.

Leery of the anger contorting the giant's face, Fred backed away from the girl. "What are you doing here?" he demanded. "You should be getting ready for your act."

"Plenty of time," Goliath replied, making no effort to leave.

Frustrated, Fred clenched his fists and turned away, just in time to see the Frenchman emerge from the corridor that led to his wife's dressing room.

Goliath and Maria could wait until he'd dealt with the foreign bastard.

~

"Excuse me, gents," Emerson warned his regulars. "I think a fight might break out any minute."

Fights weren't unusual in the music hall. People drank too much and tempers frayed. However, he'd seen the ugly glint in Fred's narrowed eyes and sensed he intended to attack the Frenchman who'd just emerged from the dressing rooms. With any luck, Fred would beat the living daylights out of the foreign upstart and he'd stay away from *The Hippodrome*. Emerson should be the man to console Maggie. Not for the first time, he wished there were some way to get rid of Fred Chadwick.

~

Edouard's first indication of trouble was the panicked expression on Foster's face. He later wished he'd paid closer attention. Next thing he knew, a fist connected with his jaw. Reeling, he tasted blood, but he'd fought in the back streets of

Paris and knew enough to duck before the next blow landed. A youth with an abusive father quickly learned how to defend himself.

Thrown off balance by a swing that missed its mark, Fred Chadwick scowled, giving Edouard an opening to land a haymaker on his opponent's nose. A satisfactory crack confirmed he'd broken the bone.

Eyes blazing anger, Chadwick raised his fists. Edouard took up a similar stance, looking forward to giving the brute a taste of his own medicine. He managed to land only one more blow to Chadwick's bloodied nose before he was restrained by the doorman.

"Get out," Chadwick screamed from the floor. "You're barred. Don't show your face here again."

"Come on," Foster urged, taking Edouard's arm. "Let's get out of here."

Edouard shrugged off the doorman's grip and complied, angry with himself as they left the premises. Barred from *The Hippodrome*, he'd forfeited the chance to ever see Maggie perform again.

"This won't do much for *Shangri-La*'s reputation," Foster muttered.

TREMBLING WITH ANGER, Fred took a kerchief from his pocket and dabbed at his nose. As pain arrowed into his head, he scowled at Emerson Dean. The waiter had offered a sweaty hand to help Fred rise, but the officious fellow was always poking his nose into matters that didn't concern him. Doubtless, he'd have some unwanted advice.

"Looks nasty. You should go to the infirmary," Dean said.

"Bugger off," Fred replied. "And I've told you a hundred

times to stop wearing so much pomade in your hair. You look ridiculous."

Jaw clenched, Emerson backed off. Fred might have known the coward wouldn't challenge his insult. A man who parted his hair down the middle and stuck it down with lashings of pomade wasn't right in the head.

Brushing himself off, he was tempted to head straight for Maggie's dressing room and punish her for this travesty. But the curiously silent crowd was watching and he was afraid he might kill his wife if he got his hands on her. Then where would he be? Dangling at the end of a rope. No, she'd get her comeuppance, but not tonight.

Instead, he slowly made his way to the rear, reassuring patrons as he went that all was well.

Goliath appeared on stage and the cheering began anew as the scantily clad giant displayed his impressive bicep muscles and began his routine. The crowd oohed and aahed as he easily lifted a dumbbell labeled 500 pounds.

Satisfied he was no longer the focus of attention, Fred slipped outside and strode down the narrow alley beside the theater. The cold air deadened the pain in his nose. The weathered door to the cellar was so innocuous, he almost missed it, though he knew it was there. Satisfied he'd wiped all the blood off his face, he squared his shoulders and knocked.

Recognized by the burly fellow who opened the door, he was welcomed into a world totally different from that of *The Hippodrome.*

After descending the stone steps, he bypassed the room used by the opium addicts and joined the rowdy crowd watching a cock fight.

Unlike the poorly dressed, malodorous millworkers around him, he wasn't interested in the blood sport, but Rajendra Bandi was addicted to it. The Indian ran this highly profitable den of iniquity, but Fred hadn't been paid his share of the profits for over a month.

As expected, he caught sight of Bandi at the front of the rabid crowd. Moving stealthily lest he spook him, he was soon standing beside his prey. "You owe me money," he said loudly, confident Bandi was hemmed in and couldn't flee. "I'll have to reconsider your tenancy here."

He wasn't sure how it happened but, suddenly, Bandi's heavies stood on either side of him. Fear crept up his spine when Bandi's dark eyes flashed. "Tha'll be paid," he hissed. "Don't threaten me agin or tha'll 'ave more than a broken nose."

Fred held up his hands in surrender. "No need to get hostile," he said before shouldering his way out through the crowd.

Back in the alley, he seethed. The setdown had doubled the pain in his nose. Bandi thought he held the upper hand, but he'd soon learn you don't cheat Fred Chadwick out of his due. Where did the Asian moron think he was going to procure his opium without Fred's contacts?

He lingered in the alley watching the happy punters file out of *The Hippodrome*. The show must be over. Maggie would be alone in her dressing room.

Satisfied all the patrons had left and the gas lights snuffed out, he made his way through the darkened hall, paying no mind to the garrulous charladies who'd already arrived to clean the place.

Stepping into the corridor that led to the dressing rooms, he caught sight of a shadowy figure lurking near the door of his office where he kept the takings under lock and key. "Oy," he shouted, in a mood to pound the would-be thief into the ground.

Chapter 4

Shangri-La

Maggie lingered in bed, nursing the hurts Fred had inflicted. Her husband often came home in the wee, small hours, but hadn't returned at all last night. He'd probably ended up in someone else's bed after visiting the opium den in the cellar he thought she knew nothing about.

She wasn't expected at the theater until mid afternoon, so there was no reason not to enjoy a lie-in without worrying about Fred's volatile temper. Her errant thoughts wandered to Edouard Deschanel. She drifted into a dream of lying naked in his arms.

Overheated and anxious to banish the long-forgotten feelings of desire coursing through her body, she flung back the sheets, rose and attended to her toilette.

Enjoying a slice of bread and strawberry jam for breakfast— a treat Fred would forbid as too fattening—she decided to while away an hour at *Shangri-La*. She convinced herself that her decision had nothing to do with the attractive Frenchman. The notion was foolhardy, but it was highly unlikely she'd bump into Fred there, or even Deschanel. The owner of such a prestigious establishment wouldn't frequent the shop floor. Fred had probably barred Deschanel from the theater after the altercation. The *Shangri-La* would be the only place she might catch a glimpse of him. Even if she didn't, the elegant department store was his world—one far removed from hers. A woman was entitled to secret dreams—obviously the reason she was intrigued by the Frenchman.

After swilling down a shot of gin, she chose a cotton day dress with a manageable bustle, a double-breasted, red wool coat, and her favorite wide-brimmed hat with its admittedly ostentatious plumes. Sturdy buttoned boots would be just the thing for the long walk from her flat on Bank Street to the far end of Deansgate.

Fred insisted she wear an uncomfortably tight corset on stage, but she decided against making the effort to do up the laces herself. No one at *Shangri-La* would be paying attention to her waist and her sore ribs needed the reprieve. She doubted the wealthy patrons of Deschanel's shop would even know who she was. Self-made men like some wealthy industrialists might frequent *The Hippodrome*, but the snobbish upper classes wouldn't be caught dead there. The prospect of shopping *incognito* was thrilling.

She paused to catch her breath at the top of the Bank Street hill and looked toward the theater. There was something going on near *The Hippodrome*—probably an argument outside *Ye Olde Man and Scythe*. The ancient pub wasn't always a good neighbor to have, even this early in the day.

She resumed her walk along Deansgate, a main thoroughfare she knew well. Today the busy street seemed different. Mucky-faced urchins rolled hoops, oblivious as usual to pedestrians. She sidestepped dubious puddles and avoided potholes. Trying to outshout each other, street vendors pedaled their wares. There was nothing unusual about her surroundings, yet the day held promise and she felt optimism for the first time in years. Arriving at the plate glass doors of *Shangri-La*, she hesitated momentarily. Perhaps this was a mistake. She didn't belong here. But the prospect of an adventure spurred her on. She filled her lungs and entered the shop, ignoring the glares of richly dressed patrons milling about inside.

She'd assumed she wouldn't be recognized, but turned up noses and cold stares from clerks drove her to follow the signs up a flight of carpeted stairs to the Ladies' Wear department.

~

It was unusual for Edouard to visit the Ladies' Wear department of his store. However, it was important he meet with the head of the department to discuss plans to display a shipment of gowns expected from the prestigious House of Worth in Paris.

Miss Eugenia Horrocks wasn't what one might consider an attractive woman. The center part in her graying hair was in fashion, yet the style made Miss Horrocks look ancient. The tight bun on top of her head didn't soften her stern appearance. In the midst of their conversation about the shipment, a snarl unexpectedly twisted the thin face into a grimace. "Of all the nerve. It's the trollop from the music hall," she hissed. "I'll get rid of her."

Edouard didn't need to turn around to know Maggie Chadwick had entered the department. His male body reacted predictably, but he kept control of his voice. "You'll do no such thing, Miss Horrocks," he replied.

He could well imagine the shock on the elderly spinster's face as he strode to greet the woman he couldn't stop thinking about. "Welcome to my humble establishment, Madame Chadwick," he said, bestowing a kiss on her knuckles. "*Bienvenue.*"

"*Mercy, monsewer,*" she tried.

He wasn't worried. He could teach her his language.

He fervently wished his own face didn't bear evidence of Chadwick's fist—until Maggie raised her hand and touched his cheek. The longing and regret in her brown eyes sent his spirits soaring. She had feelings for him.

But there was no hope of a future with her as long as she was married to the brute. "What can we interest you in today?" he asked, hoping she'd come expressly to see him and not explore his store. "A new gown, perhaps?"

"Perhaps," she allowed, looking straight into his eyes. "I might be more interested in a guided tour of your store, and please call me Maggie."

She was flirting with him. It was dangerous, but he loved it. "And I'm Edouard. It would be my pleasure," he replied, gently putting his arm around her waist. He could tell immediately that she wasn't wearing a corset. His body rejoiced as carnal thoughts ran rampant.

Foster Marsh chewed his lower lip. He was proud of his prestigious position as the manager at *Shangri-La* and had enormous respect for Edouard Deschanel. The man knew more about retailing than anyone he'd ever met in his ten year career in smaller shops. Foster had initially harbored reservations about the notion of establishing a luxury department store in his native Bolton, but Deschanel had a flair for display. Patrons loved it and the store was thriving.

However, his boss's preoccupation with Maggie Chadwick worried him. He'd hoped the altercation at the theater might have dampened Edouard's enthusiasm, but here he was, fawning over a music-hall performer who certainly wasn't the kind of client they wanted to encourage. It didn't bode well, especially if Fred Chadwick got wind of it. He felt only sympathy for a woman married to a man with a reputation as a vicious bully and womanizer. Not to mention rumors of his criminality. Edouard would be well advised to steer clear of Maggie Chadwick.

~

THE WARMTH of Edouard's arm penetrated even the wool of Maggie's coat. His firm support was exhilarating, but she was relieved when he offered his arm instead as they embarked on the tour. His careful touch indicated he was aware of her painful ribs, but walking arm in arm was more appropriate. Some women did recognize her as she strolled around *Shangri-La* escorted by the proprietor. The disapproval in their haughty regard was unmistakable. The well-to-do would misjudge her motive for befriending Edouard. Tongues would wag. Fred would soon hear gossip about the floozy from the music hall swanning about *Shangri-La* on the arm of the proprietor. She would pay dearly for this transgression, but she didn't care.

A thrill stole up her spine when her escort dabbed expensive scent on her wrist at the perfume counter, though she worried he might uncover the bruises. She was tempted to accept his offer to purchase for her a darling atomizer filled with an intoxicating perfume she'd never heard of, but Fred would grill her mercilessly until she tearfully confessed where she'd obtained it. Her husband had his ways of extorting the truth.

When they stopped by the department selling chronometers, her guide's explanation of the inner workings of the wondrous pocket watches held her spellbound. Surrounded by luxury and comfortable being escorted by a handsome man she liked immensely, she felt happier than she had in many a year.

The wonderful store even had a café where she and

Edouard enjoyed a delicious lunch of baked brie and fresh bread. "Tell me how you came to be involved in opening a luxury store," she said, anxious to know more about him.

"*Bien*, I was born in a small rural village in Provence, but I acquired my retailing expertise at the *Bon Marché* in Paris where I worked for almost five years. When Aristide and Marguerite Boucicaut took over the famous store, they revolutionized retail by combining luxury and availability. The shop offered an extensive selection of goods, from fashion to home decor, and featured fixed prices."

"That's a big change. Here, people are used to haggling."

"In France too, but the store's grand architecture and artful displays attracted shoppers from all over the world. I loved it and Marguerite saw my potential. I was quickly promoted from junior clerk to management."

"And did you like Paris?"

"The city taught me many things, including how to spot men and women with evil intent."

"But you left Paris."

"The Boucicauts sent me to manage *Arcadia*, the *Bon Marché's* first foray into England. That brought me into contact with the best and worst of wealthy Englishmen."

"How long were you in London?"

"Two years, but I'm not a fan of big city life, so I offered to invest my own funds in the company's first north of England venture and the Boucicauts backed me willingly. I found this old building on Deansgate and decided it was perfect for *Shangri-La*. It has an elegant facade, wonderfully ornate interior design and could be converted to provide enough floor space to create an inviting shopping experience."

"You certainly offer a great array of goods, from high-end fashion to lovely home furnishings."

"We endeavor to provide a place where shoppers can find

everything they need, and we give our customers personalized attention. Our staff are trained to cater to the needs of our wealthy clientele."

Seeking to prolong the first intelligent conversation she'd had in years, she remarked on the window displays. "The displays in your windows are so elaborate and inviting."

Excited by his beguiling eyes and flared nostrils, she sipped the last of her wine. The glass of French wine was probably a mistake. She could tolerate gin, but the wine had gone straight to her head. "I should be getting back to *The Hippodrome*," she said, aware she was slurring her words.

Edouard laughed, his dark eyes full of merriment. She laughed with him.

"Allow me to escort you," he said, pulling out the chair so she could rise, a courtesy that had never occurred to Fred.

As they left the store arm in arm, she worried that passersby could tell she was tipsy.

By the time they reached Churchgate, her head had cleared. Fresh air, a brisk walk, and light-hearted conversation with an attractive man had done the trick. However, she stopped abruptly when they arrived at *The Hippodrome*. Her fellow performers were part of a crowd that had gathered outside. Goliath shielded Maria in his arms. Emerson sat on the ground, his greasy head in his hands. Smoking a cigarette, the third-rate comedian Fred had hired the previous week leaned on the wall. The others formed a silent group. A uniformed constable guarded the door. Despite the stovepipe hat, she recognized him as a regular punter from the gallery. "What's going on?" she asked the policeman, hastily unhooking her arm from Edouard's.

"Yer 'usband's bin found dead, Mrs. Chadwick," he replied, eyeing her escort with undisguised censure.

Deschanel broke her fall when her knees buckled. Leaning

on his strength, she didn't know whether to laugh or cry. Fred was dead. She was free.

"How did he die?" Deschanel asked.

"Garroted, Sir. Gruesome business. Inspector 'Alliwell is inside with the body. I assume 'e'll want to speak to Mrs. Chadwick."

Legs trembling and stomach churning, Maggie grappled to comprehend the incredible—someone had murdered Fred. She couldn't say who might have committed the crime. Fred offended almost everyone he met and probably had many enemies, but suspicion was bound to fall on her—and Deschanel. "Go," she told him. "Quickly."

EMERSON SUPPOSED he should be horrified. Fred had apparently died a violent death. However—"Live by the sword, die by the sword," he muttered, glad for Maggie's sake the tyrant was gone for good.

Now, he only had to get rid of the Frenchman who'd just escorted Maggie to the theater. Good thing Fred was dead. He'd have been livid if he knew his wife had spent time with the foreigner. The absurd notion brought a rare smile to Emerson's face. It was curious, and perhaps telling, that the frog had beaten a hasty retreat when told of the murder. In time, Maggie would see Emerson was the man she could rely on.

Chapter 5

Brutal Murder

Inspector Marcus Halliwell removed his stovepipe hat, tucked it under his arm, and hunkered down beside the twisted body. As a constable, he'd patrolled the dark streets of Bolton's town center for many years before his promotion. It was still early morning and the cluttered room was dimly lit, but he immediately recognized the victim. "You've crossed somebody once too often, Chadwick," he murmured.

Notebook and pencil in hand, Constable Walsh bent closer. "Sorry, Sir, I didn't catch that."

Halliwell sighed. Walsh was keen and clever, but the Superintendent's decision to assign a raw recruit as Marcus' assistant spoke volumes about a lack of confidence in his newly promoted inspector. As a sergeant, Marcus had solved the murder of a boy at Broadclough Mills. The arrest of the perpetrator had been brought about more by good luck than good detective work, but still ... It would take more than luck to prove himself worthy of the promotion. Finding Chadwick's killer would be a challenge. The man was universally feared and disliked.

It wouldn't help Marcus' reputation if Walsh recorded

words spoken to a dead man. "His nose is broken, and the garrote cut into his Adam's apple," he said, pointing to Chadwick's crushed throat.

"That would take strength," Walsh replied. "We're probably looking for a man."

Marcus clenched his jaw as he stood. "We can't jump to conclusions, Constable."

"No, Sir," Walsh replied sheepishly.

"But you could be right," Marcus allowed, scanning the room for any clues. "I don't see the weapon."

"Something thin and sharp," Walsh suggested. "Like wire, perhaps."

"Possibly, though I doubt the killer would have left it behind."

"This is a dressing room, I suppose," Walsh said, following his superior's gaze.

"Mrs. Chadwick's, I'd say, judging by the rack of costumes and the cosmetics. As top of the bill and the owner's wife, she's probably the only performer with a private dressing room."

"No signs of a struggle," Walsh observed.

Marcus nodded. "What do you think that signifies?"

"The murderer burst in and surprised him."

"Likely, or he knew his killer and didn't expect an attack."

"Could his wife be responsible?"

"It's possible, though I doubt she'd kill him in her own dressing room, and does she have the strength required?"

"Unless it began as an argument and she had help."

"It's a possibility," Marcus agreed. "One thing is for sure. Few will mourn this wretch."

"A bad lot, was he, sir?"

"You could say that," Marcus replied, startled when the door was thrust open and a stunningly beautiful woman dithered on the threshold. She stared, transfixed by the sight of the grotesque corpse on the floor.

"Sorry, Sir," a red-faced Constable Martin declared from the corridor. "I couldn't stop Mrs. Chadwick."

So, this was the famous Miss Maggie, darling of the common people. Marcus hurried to escort the widow out of the room. The color had drained from her face. She seemed to be in shock, but he had best remember she was a seasoned performer. "You shouldn't be here, Mrs. Chadwick," he said. "Constable Martin will escort you home. I'd ask you to stay there until I have a chance to finish up here."

"Of course," she replied. "Do you know who's responsible?"

For the newly bereaved widow of a brutally murdered man, she was too calm. There were no tears, but then it was common knowledge Chadwick beat his wife. That alone gave her a motive for murder.

After she left, Marcus hunkered down beside the body again and sniffed. At first, he'd smelled only blood and gin. Now, there was a faint trace of something else.

"What do you smell, Sir?" Walsh asked.

"Opium, my boy," he replied. "Let's speak with the char who found the body."

~

EDOUARD WAS HALFWAY BACK to *Shangri-La* when the shock wore off. He couldn't let Maggie cope with this trauma alone. He stopped to consider what he should do next. He'd always been a decisive man, but these were unusual circumstances and he felt uncomfortable dithering in a busy public street. He'd already attracted the curious attention of several passersby.

Fred Chadwick had been garroted. Maggie confessed over

lunch that she no longer loved the brute, but that didn't mean she felt nothing. A grizzly murder wasn't something a person shrugged off. It would be crass to begin his courtship too soon but he could offer sympathy, a shoulder to cry on.

He retraced his steps as far as the market cross on Churchgate before it struck him he didn't know where Maggie might have ended up. Was she still in the nearby theater or had she been taken somewhere for questioning?

He knew she wasn't capable of murder, but she'd be a prime suspect.

His gut clenched when it dawned on him that he too would come under suspicion. He'd fought with Fred Chadwick in front of multiple witnesses. Many of his wealthy patrons had seen him and Maggie getting along famously at *Shangri-La*. As soon as news spread about the murder, rumors would swirl about a romance between them. Bolton wasn't like Paris. There was no anonymity. He'd voiced his admiration for her and his defiant resentment of her husband's brutality. Worse still, his dubious past would eventually come to light.

~

"LIKE I SAID," Hilda Smith told Marcus. "I were just startin' on dumpin' out the ashtrays when I saw Mr. Chadwick cross the floor and 'ead for the corridor to the dressin' rooms. Then I 'eard 'im shout '*Oy*.'"

"Oy?" Marcus repeated. "He saw someone?"

"Mebbe somebody 'e didn't expect to see there, I s'pose," Hilda replied, poking a finger to scratch inside the ragged turban knotted around her hair.

Walsh licked the end of his pencil. "Did you see anybody emerge from the corridor?" he asked.

Marcus glared at his assistant. He was leading this investigation and the new recruit had best remember it.

"Not reet away," Hilda replied. "Truth be told, I weren't really payin' attention and most ov the lights 'ad bin dimmed as usual. There were folk comin' and goin'. A few stragglers from the gallery. Some o' the turns came out from the dressin' rooms."

Walsh remained silent, so Marcus asked the next question. The constable seemed to have got the unspoken message that Inspector Marcus Halliwell was in charge. "Anyone in particular you recall?"

"Let me think," she mused, scratching again. "Goliath, the strongman ... the new, so-called comedian ... the cigarette girl ... the waiter ... some of the musicians from the pit."

Marcus began to see the advantage of having Walsh jot down all this information. "Not Mrs. Chadwick?" he asked.

"No, she would have left earlier."

"Why do you say that?"

"Well, she's always gone by t' time I get to work."

"So, you didn't see Mrs. Chadwick last night at all?"

"No. Can I go now? I'm usually 'ome long before this. George'll wonder what's become o' me. He gets suspicious, tha knows."

"Just one more thing. What time did you discover the body?"

"Well, I do the dressin' rooms last, after the lavatories. And I had to sweep up the pieces of a broken gin bottle in the corridor. The lavs take some work, let me tell thee. Especially the men, they ..."

"Yes, Mrs. Smith, we understand," Marcus said, anxious to be done with the garrulous woman. "If you can just tell us what time you discovered the body."

Hilda pouted. "Well, I s'pose it must have been about six

o'clock, give or take. It were a nasty shock findin' 'im like that. I came over quite faint."

"But you didn't touch anything?"

"Not likely. I ran out screamin'. Frightened the life out o' Agnes. She's t' other char. We rushed outside to find a copper. Took ages before one came by."

"Thank you, Mrs. Smith," Marcus said, mentally crossing her off the list of suspects. "One last thing. Did you see where Mr. Chadwick came from when he entered the hall?"

"I thought 'e'd been outside. 'E looked cold."

"So you didn't see him arguing with anyone before he crossed the hall?"

"No, but I 'eard there were a bit of a donnybrook earlier in the evening."

"A donnybrook?" Walsh asked, apparently unsure how to record the information.

"Tha' knows. Fisticuffs. Mr. Chadwick and that French feller from the posh shop on Deansgate. The frog broke 'is schnoz by all accounts."

"*Shangri-La?*"

"Aye, 'im."

Marcus added a possibility to the list of suspects. The fight explained the broken nose, but why had Chadwick been outside?

Edouard was about to approach the policeman outside *The Hippodrome* when two more uniformed men emerged from the theater. One was slightly older and the tallest man Edouard had ever seen. He could be the inspector in charge of investigating the murder.

He had a sinking feeling his presence might be deemed

suspicious. The crowd had disappeared, so the policemen couldn't fail to notice him. Hurrying away would make things worse.

"This 'ere's the chap what escorted Mrs. Chadwick, Sir," the constable on guard duty said.

Experience and the fact he was innocent of any crime cleared Edouard's head. "Edouard Deschanel," he declared, offering his hand to the older of the two newcomers. "Proprietor of *Shangri-La* on Deansgate."

"Inspector Halliwell," the policeman replied, ignoring the offer of a handshake. "My assistant is Constable Walsh. Were you acquainted with Mr. Chadwick?"

"Well, not exactly acquainted," Edouard replied, pointing to the cut on his lip. "We had a disagreement yesterday."

"A disagreement that resulted in a fight and Mr. Chadwick suffering a broken nose, I understand."

"Yes, he apparently took exception to something I did and attacked me in front of everyone in the music hall."

"And why do you think he was angry? Something to do with Mrs. Chadwick perhaps?"

Edouard decided honesty was the best policy, though that hadn't always held true for him. "I'm an admirer. I visited her dressing room. He probably didn't like that."

"And you arrived here today with Mrs. Chadwick."

"Yes, she requested a tour of my store. I was happy to oblige and it would have been ungentlemanly to allow her to walk here alone."

When the inspector made no reply, Edouard risked a glance at the assistant who'd been furiously writing in a notebook. As if sensing he was being watched, Walsh looked up. Edouard didn't like the censure in the young man's narrowed eyes. The constable thought him guilty. He hurriedly racked his brain for something to say that would shift suspicion away from him.

Finally, it came to him. "I was remiss in not offering Mrs. Chadwick my condolences. The shock of the news, I suppose. I'd like to make up for the thoughtless oversight. Can you provide me with her direction?"

If he didn't even know where the widow lived, how could he be accused of involvement in a plot to kill her husband?

Apprised of the address, he took his leave and set off for Bank Street, unable to untie the knot of foreboding in his belly.

Chapter 6

A Sordid Past

"Was it wise to tell Deschanel that Mrs. Chadwick lives on Bank Street?" Walsh asked.

Marcus bristled. He didn't appreciate a subordinate questioning his decisions. "He may already know that."

"But he said ..."

"People lie, Walsh. You can't automatically take what they say as the truth. In any case, if he didn't know where she lives, any Tom, Dick or Harry on the street could probably tell him she lives around the corner from Churchgate."

"Do you think he did it?"

Marcus pondered the facts. "He and the victim fought. He's clearly enamored with Maggie Chadwick. The garrote is a weapon favored by the French."

"Guilty then."

"It would be easy to assume that, wouldn't it?"

"But you don't think so, Sir."

"Let's reserve judgment."

~

Heartsick, Maggie paced the confines of her dingy flat. The peeling wallpaper and threadbare rugs spoke of years of neglect. She'd long since given up the effort to make their home comfortable and Fred didn't give a damn about the place. She'd endured too much abuse at the hands of her husband here. Even in death, he reached out to threaten her. It was inevitable that suspicion would fall on her and Edouard, a gentleman who'd shown her nothing but kindness. The realization she might never be free tightened her throat.

Rummaging in her wardrobe, she retrieved the hidden gin bottle, pulled out the stopper and took a gulp. When she'd first turned to drink, the blue ruin had deadened the pain. Now, it made her headache worse, burned her throat and made her cough.

Sitting on the edge of the bed, she espied the garments sewn hastily by the theater's part-time seamstress after her mother's death. Not yet certain of her mixed feelings about Fred's demise, she nevertheless realized she would have to dress in mourning for a suitable period. People expected it.

Fifteen minutes later, she studied her appearance in the mirror. The black Garibaldi blouse was a little out of fashion, but it would have to do, as would the pleated black bombazine skirt. She dug her black lambs wool coat out of the back of the wardrobe and hung it on the door handle to air. She owned a black bonnet, but finding it would have to wait. Unexpected tears welled as she stared at her sober reflection. Her throat tightened. Life with Fred had never been easy, but she sensed things were about to get even more difficult. With one murderous act, the killer had at once freed her and put her future at risk.

Over and over, she rehearsed her answers to the questions the police would ask when they came, but she'd returned home alone after Edouard's visit to her dressing room and Fred's subsequent attack. She'd slipped out by the rear entrance, nervous about the commotion going on in the hall. There had been no mistaking Fred's angry voice. However, no one could verify that she'd fled alone.

Would it be better to say she'd spent the night with Edouard? She wished with all her heart that were true, but couldn't implicate him in a lie. She was developing feelings for the Frenchman she hadn't felt for anyone in a long time, but he'd probably lost interest in a woman who stank of gin. She knew almost nothing about him. Where had he gone after the fight with Fred? Perhaps he'd remained concealed in the hall and ...

A tap at the door dragged her off the dark path her thoughts had taken. "Who is it?" she asked, expecting Halliwell's voice.

"Edouard. May I enter?"

She hid the gin bottle and hurried to let him in, reassured by the welcome sound of his deep voice that he was no murderer. As soon as she saw the concern in his eyes, she threw caution to the wind and melted into his embrace, holding her breath lest he detect the odor of spirits.

They swayed together in the open doorway. Maggie felt safe, held tight in his strong arms—until Halliwell and his constable loomed large in the narrow stairwell. The policemen could draw only one conclusion.

"I see you found Mrs. Chadwick," Walsh said to the Frenchman.

The heavy sarcasm in the constable's voice irritated Marcus. A policeman had to deal in facts, not supposition.

Mrs. Chadwick's fierce blush might indicate feelings of guilt, but Marcus suspected it was caused by embarrassment at being caught in another man's arms shortly after her husband's death. Deschanel was perhaps simply a compassionate man who'd come to offer condolences, as he claimed.

Every policeman in Bolton was aware of Fred Chadwick's violent temper and dubious reputation—always one step ahead of the law. His involvement in criminal enterprises could never be proven. Witnesses either disappeared or refused to testify.

Marcus surmised his wife had learned the hard way never to provoke her husband. Sympathy welled up in his throat. She'd lived in fear for years, yet was already wearing mourning clothes for a man who brutalized her. He couldn't abide men who abused women, especially ones they were supposed to love and protect. If he and Eliza had married …

"Please," Maggie said, interrupting his wandering thoughts as she stepped away from Deschanel. "Do come in. All of you."

She evidently wanted the Frenchman present during the interview. Marcus decided not to read too much into that. Perhaps they needed to get their stories straight, or she simply craved support at a difficult time.

When she bade them be seated, Deschanel seemed hesitant —possibly an indication he'd never been in the flat before. Mrs. Chadwick would be playing with fire if she entertained other men in Fred's lair. In the event, Marcus sat on the threadbare settee, Walsh perched on a wooden stool and Deschanel remained standing.

Seeking to lessen the tension, Marcus told Mrs. Chadwick, "I remember your father."

"You would, of course," she replied with a shrug. "He was something of a firebrand in the trade union movement."

Marcus had hoped to put her at ease but had succeeded in

ruffling her feathers. "Well, those men were simply campaigning for better wages and safer working conditions."

"I suppose. Would you gentlemen like tea?"

Marcus gladly accepted the offer. When Mrs. Chadwick retreated to the kitchenette, it gave him an opportunity to size up Deschanel again. "How's your new store faring, *Monsieur?*" he asked.

Clearly taken off guard by the question, the Frenchman dragged his eyes away from Mrs. Chadwick and frowned. "Very well. Better than expected, in fact."

"I'm surprised," Marcus confessed. "I wouldn't have thought Bolton a good location for such an expensive store."

"The principals of *Le Bon Marché* did a great deal of research before deciding on a northern location. There are many wealthy families in this town who do not think my goods are expensive."

"The *nouveau riche* industrialists," Walsh hissed.

Marcus worried. Men who'd made their fortunes in industry and mining had brought wealth and prosperity to Lancashire. He admired mill owners like Roger Sandiford with whom he'd become acquainted in the course of his first murder investigation. The master of Broadclough Mill paid decent wages. He and his wife were doing their utmost to provide relief for workers laid off because of the current cotton famine.

Yet, Walsh seemed resentful of the industrialists' success. Marcus had to ponder the reason for his antipathy, but Deschanel's wry smile led him to believe it wasn't the first time the man had dealt with the same working class prejudices.

"I'm a simple storekeeper," the Frenchman replied. "I endeavor to give my patrons what they want."

"And why did Mrs. Chadwick want a tour?"

Deschanel shrugged. "Why does any beautiful woman want to enjoy the luxuries to be found at *Shangri-La?*"

Marcus had to admit the Frenchman was slick. He'd wager the Parisian had dealt with law enforcement before. Too bad there was no way to find out about his background—except to ask directly. "Ever been arrested?" he asked.

❧

Again, Edouard was torn. Revealing his regrettable past would throw suspicion on him. However, in his experience, lies usually came back to haunt the liar. "Twice, in fact, Inspector."

"Care to explain?"

Edouard's hope that Maggie Chadwick wouldn't hear his confession was dashed when she returned with the tea tray. Seeing her garbed in black brought back memories he'd sooner forget. "I was fifteen when my father beat my mother to death in a drunken rage," he said, not surprised when shock widened her eyes. "I found *Maman's* body, tracked my father down to the local bar and thrashed him to within an inch of his life."

"You were then arrested."

"*Oui*, but I was pardoned after they hanged my father. We Frenchmen respect courage. I was afraid to tell them it was anger, and perhaps fear, that drove me to beat him, not courage."

"So, you get violent when you are angry?" the inspector asked. "Is that what happened with the second arrest?"

Edouard wished with all his heart he didn't have to reveal more sordid details of his life in France. "No, I was accused of murdering my wife."

Maggie swayed as the color drained from her face.

"And did you?" the policeman asked.

He shook his head, willing away the terrible memories. "It was quickly proven that a lover killed her. Some sort of unintended accident involving his cravat during a lovemaking episode. He took his own life when he realized what he'd done. He left a note expressing his deep regret."

Complete silence greeted this account until Halliwell spoke. "With your checkered past, I'm somewhat surprised the owners of your store trusted you to manage *Shangri-La.*"

"Ah, Inspector, you demonstrate a lack of understanding of the retail trade. *Bon Marché* recognized me as a risk taker, an essential quality in an entrepreneur. In addition, I must inform you that I am the majority owner of *Shangri-La.*"

SHOCKED to the core by Edouard Deschanel's revelations, Maggie remained standing, not quite sure what to do with the tea tray. If she held on to it much longer, her trembling arms might let it fall to the floor.

Edouard came to her aid. "Allow me," he said bestowing a reassuring smile as he took the tray from her and placed it on the occasional table. "Would you like me to pour?"

She'd tried to deny she was falling in love with this incredible man who'd borne so much tragedy, but now she was free to give rein to her burgeoning feelings. "Please," she replied with a broad smile, hoping he understood she didn't censure him for the misfortunes he had suffered.

She suspected his emotions were in turmoil, yet he poured and served the tea with a steady hand, politely asking the policemen if they preferred one lump of sugar or two.

Even standing with a dainty cup and saucer in his hand, he looked composed and confident. She refused a cup of tea, afraid the china cup would rattle on the saucer. After sipping his tea, Halliwell complimented her on its strength. Walsh stared into his tea as if he feared it might be poisoned.

"So," Halliwell said after accepting the offer of a second

cup. "I'd appreciate it if you could detail your movements last evening, Mrs. Chadwick."

Walsh hastily placed his cup and saucer on the table and took out his notebook and pencil, his confidence seemingly restored. Maggie might have imagined it, but a trace of a smile tugged at the corners of Halliwell's mouth. She decided she liked this inspector.

"I heard the commotion in the hall," she began. "As you know, fighting isn't unknown in music halls."

Halliwell nodded.

"My husband's strident voice indicated he was involved."

"Did you hear anyone else's voice?"

"No, but I suspected Fred was fighting with Mr. Deschanel."

"Why?"

Edouard cleared his throat as he put down his cup and saucer. "Because I had just left her dressing room."

Maggie rushed to clear waters that were becoming muddied. "One of the drawbacks of being popular," she said. "Members of the audience frequently come to ask for my autograph."

"That wasn't the purpose of my visit," Edouard asserted. "I recognize the traits of an abuser when I see them, and I knew Chadwick had abused his wife."

"Is that true?" Halliwell asked.

Maggie drew back her sleeve to reveal the bruises on her arm. "Yes. Fred could be violent."

"And what transpired between the two of you in the dressing room?"

"Nothing untoward, I assure you," Maggie retorted.

"I told her I wouldn't allow him to continue his beatings," Edouard admitted.

"Why should you care?" Walsh asked derisively. "She's just a music hall vamp."

Maggie bristled.

Edouard fisted his hands.

"That's quite enough, Constable," Halliwell interjected. "You'll apologize to Mrs. Chadwick."

"Sorry," Walsh muttered.

"I apologize for my constable's rudeness," the Inspector said. "However, Mr. Deschanel, why do you care what happens to Mrs. Chadwick?"

"Because she's a beautiful and talented woman," Edouard replied.

Maggie's hopes rose. Deschanel had feelings for her. Then, hope faltered when he said, "Any man who stands by and does nothing to protect a vulnerable woman isn't a man."

"I think that's all for now," Halliwell said as he stood. "Thanks for the tea."

Both policemen were halfway out the door when the Inspector turned to her. "One more thing, Mrs. Chadwick. Was your husband an opium addict?"

"WHAT'S YOUR OPINION?" Marcus asked his constable when they reached the street.

"Guilty as sin, both of them," Walsh replied.

Marcus wasn't surprised his young assistant had jumped to that conclusion. For himself, he wasn't so sure. The pair hadn't gone so far as to admit they were lovers, or in love at any rate, but they'd been forthright in answering his questions. Deschanel had voluntarily revealed his past knowing it was unlikely a Bolton policeman would have access to Paris records.

"Surely you agree, sir," Walsh said.

Marcus secured his hat back on his head. "Let's see about finding a way into this opium den Mrs. Chadwick seems to think operates in the cellars."

"An opium den in Bolton?" Walsh exclaimed with incredulity. "A lie if ever I heard one."

"You're too naive," Marcus replied.

Chapter 7

Namaste

Marcus and his constable walked slowly down the alley alongside *The Hippodrome*. There were several decrepit doors on either side but only one looked like it might have been used recently.

"This could be it," Marcus told Walsh. "I think we'd better send for reinforcements. If Mrs. Chadwick is right about an opium den, I don't fancy our chances if we go in alone."

Eyes as big as saucers, Walsh jumped backwards when the door in question opened without warning. The sill dragged on the stone step, giving Marcus a chance to recover his wits. It wouldn't do to look startled in front of Walsh, especially when a diminutive East Indian man dressed in business attire and top hat emerged, stepped into the alley and bowed.

"*Baap re baap*," he exclaimed in a sing-song accent. "Forgive me for calling upon the divine, but I'm relieved to see you gentlemen of the law. Rajendra Bandi at your service. Come in, come in."

Marcus hesitated. There was something odd about the man, though he couldn't put his finger on what it was. Apparently recovered from his shock, Walsh marched right into the cellar and took out his notebook.

Marcus stared at the dozens of cardboard boxes piled almost to the ceiling. Somebody had gone to a lot of trouble to make them think the cellar was simply a warehouse, but the sweet smell of smoked opium lingered.

"When I heard about the murder, I was worried about my merchandise," Bandi said as he opened a box and took out a handful of miniature Union Jacks.

Walsh leaned close to Marcus' ear. "Nothing here, sir, except a wog and his stuff for Tuesday's market stall."

Reaching for one of the flags, Marcus shook his head. "Very nice, Mr. Bandi. I'll wager such a patriotic gentleman as yourself is from India."

Bandi quickly hid the surprise that flashed in his dark eyes. "You'd be partially right, *Sahib*. My grandparents worked for a British major in India and, at his request, came to England with him when his tour of duty was over."

It was a familiar tale, one Marcus had heard more than once. However, most of the Indian families he knew ran prosperous, legitimate businesses in the clothing industry. Children of the third generation born in Lancashire didn't usually speak with an Indian accent and use the subservient *Sahib*. Bandi was trying hard to give the wrong impression of who and what he was. The marketing of tawdry souvenirs was not a trade East Indians normally participated in.

And then there were the lingering odors. Not just opium. Blood. And the rank odor of too many sweaty men in a confined space. Not to mention the flag smelled musty.

"You're no doubt aware there's been a murder upstairs. Did you know the victim?" he asked.

Bandi tsked sorrowfully. "Yes, I heard. Once a month, I

went to Mr. Chadwick's office to pay rent, you understand. Terrible business. Have you arrested the culprit?"

"No," Walsh replied. "But we have our prime suspects."

Marcus rolled his eyes. "We are in the process of eliminating people. Can you account for your whereabouts the night of the murder?" he asked.

"Oh, yes, *Sahib*. I was celebrating Rama Navami with fellow Hindus. It is a festival that celebrates the birth of Rama, one of the most popularly revered deities in Hinduism, also known as the seventh avatar of Vishnu. He is often held as an emblem within Hinduism for being an ideal king and human through his righteousness, good conduct and virtue."

Marcus nodded thoughtfully. The well-rehearsed alibi rolled off Bandi's glib tongue too easily, and he'd taken measures to convince the police there was nothing dodgy going on beneath *The Hippodrome*. "Thank you for your help, Mr. Bandi. We'll be off," he said, chivvying Walsh to the steps.

"*Namaste*," Bandi replied affecting the correct respectful pose.

"Just one more thing," Marcus said. "How long have you been renting this space?"

"Not long," Bandi replied.

Back in the street, Marcus handed his flag to Walsh. "What's your opinion?"

"Seems harmless enough, sir," he replied, waving the little flag.

"Did you smell anything unusual?"

"Smell, sir? I don't understand."

"So, you didn't write down that the place reeks of opium and blood?"

The red-faced Walsh looked so crestfallen as he scribbled in his notebook that Marcus almost felt sorry for him. But the young constable had to learn. "Give the flag a sniff," he commanded.

"Musty, sir," Walsh replied after complying. "Been in storage a long time."

"Make a note of that, Constable."

RAJENDRA HAD ANTICIPATED the murder would bring policemen to the theater. He'd immediately put a stop to the cockfights. The opium smokers rarely left the premises alive, so that income was secure. However, he'd realized it was simply a matter of time before the police discovered the cellar was occupied, and had prepared for the eventuality. The door to the opium den was nailed shut and boarded over. The addicts within wouldn't care or even notice. He'd left them a goodly supply of the drug. All traces of the hay bales used around the pit where dogs fought to the death, had been removed, and the floor scrubbed.

His men had filled the space with cartons of Union Jacks and red, white and blue bunting brought from a warehouse he rented near the River Croal. He'd purchased and stored the patriotic paraphernalia for just such an emergency. The theater above was dark out of respect for the owner's death. Churchgate was quiet at night except for the regulars spilling out of *Ye Olde Man and Scythe* and they were too drunk to notice anything.

Rajendra was no longer obliged to pay rent and split the profits with Chadwick, something he'd long resented having to do. Never again would he have to travel to Liverpool with his landlord to take delivery of the opium he needed. He'd soon find new contacts in India to replace Chadwick's. He'd no longer be obliged to endure the man's apparent need to sleep with every woman they encountered on the way there and back. As for the incessant bragging about his sexual prowess …

It was unlikely Fred's actress wife would take over running the theater. Women didn't know the first thing about operating a business and Rajendra would never trust a woman as a partner. That raised the possibility of the theater being sold. A new owner might not take kindly to having a criminal enterprise in the cellar, but most people could be swayed by the amount of money to be made. If not, he'd soon track down another suitable location.

Rajendra felt satisfied he'd pulled the wool over the policemen's eyes. As he'd hoped, the murder was working to his advantage. Life would be easier without Fred Chadwick sticking his nose into Rajendra's business. He sensed both coppers suspected him simply because he was dark-skinned. Being born and bred in Lancashire never counted for anything. Providing himself with an alibi had been a masterful move. He hoped he hadn't laid the Indian accent on too thick.

"Do you think the wog is the killer, Sir?" Walsh asked as they walked back to the street.

"First of all, Walsh, Bandi isn't a *wog*, he was born here."

"But you can't trust any of those dark-skinned fellows," the constable replied. "I'd a mate killed in the Sepoy Mutiny a few years ago. Bright young chap he was."

Marcus had a feeling Bandi wouldn't have a clue what you were talking about if you mentioned the Sepoy Mutiny, but it probably wasn't worth the effort to try to overcome Walsh's prejudices. "There's no doubt Bandi's hiding something illegal, but killing Chadwick would bring attention I'm sure he'd rather do without."

"I suppose you're right," Walsh allowed. "Fixing up the cellar like that must have taken a lot of work."

"And, *The Hippodrome* is in limbo now without Chadwick at the helm. Bandi might have to find some other unscrupulous landlord willing to provide a place to run his operation."

"So, should we cross him off the list of suspects?"

"Not just yet," Marcus replied, unwilling to admit Edouard Deschanel was looking like a more likely culprit.

Chapter 8

Hasty Burial

"Thank you for coming with me," Maggie said nervously as she and Edouard sat in the waiting room of Stillett's Funeral Parlor. She was worried that the police had consigned Fred's body to the most expensive undertakers in town.

He raised their joined hands to his lips. "Think nothing of it."

She startled when a tall man entered and introduced himself. Surprised by his appearance, she paid scant attention to his name. If she'd been casting someone as an undertaker in a skit, she'd have chosen this fellow. He was slightly stooped, balding, and had a hooked nose.

"How may we be of service?" he asked, wringing his hands.

"Mrs. Chadwick is recently widowed," Edouard explained.

"Ah, yes, the murder at the theater," he replied. "You'll require our finest coffin."

Maggie was torn. Would people think less of her if she chose a simple coffin? Where was she to find the funds for such an expense?

"No," Edouard replied, handing over his business card.

"Something simple, and send your invoice to my attention at *Shangri-La*."

"Of course, Mr. Deschanel," the obsequious fellow replied. "I can also see to purchasing a plot at Tonge if Mrs. Chadwick wishes."

Maggie could only nod. She was relieved Edouard had taken charge, but she couldn't allow him to pay for the funeral and told him so after they left.

"I will do whatever is required to make life easier for you," he replied, taking hold of her hands. "It's the least I can do. You've already enriched my life."

Marcus began to see the advantage of having a younger man as an assistant. Tonge Cemetery, site of Chadwick's burial, was a fair distance from town. Marcus insisted he could have managed the quadricycle himself but quickly deferred to Walsh's offer to take over the pedaling of the four-wheeled contraption.

The Superintendent agreed with Marcus' assertion he should attend the interment and had magnanimously allowed the use of the Bolton Borough police force's latest means of transportation which was an improvement over the penny farthing, an invention Marcus had never mastered.

All he had to do with the quadricycle was sit in the front seat between the two big wheels, yet he was winded by the time they reached the cemetery. He attributed his breathlessness to helping push the contraption up the occasional steep hill. However, Walsh was barely out of breath. They left the cycle at the entrance to the cemetery.

Sidestepping gravestones, Marcus unexpectedly felt the full weight of his thirty years. He supposed he should be glad he'd survived ten years as a policeman. Most died on the job, were dismissed for drunkenness or quit within a year of joining the force. He was proud to be a policeman and fervently hoped he would manage to solve this murder. If not, he'd likely be demoted back to the rank of sergeant and expected to once again pound the beat.

The horse-drawn hearse passed them as they walked. Behind it came a stylish carriage from which Edouard Deschanel emerged. He turned to assist Maggie Chadwick to alight. Marcus had a feeling the elegantly dressed Frenchman probably owned the carriage and the sleek horse in the traces.

As expected, Mrs. Chadwick was garbed in black from head to toe. Marcus privately thought the feathers of her hat were somewhat ostentatious for the occasion, but who could blame the woman? Fred Chadwick was no great loss.

However, murder was a crime and Marcus would see justice done, no matter how much sympathy he felt for the killer.

A motley crew dribbled into the cemetery, black armbands around their sleeves. Presumably they'd walked from town. Marcus recognized them as other employees from *The Hippodrome*. "We'll need to question this lot," he told Walsh.

Two undertakers took off their top hats as they climbed down from the driver's seat of the hearse and opened the rear door. Two gravediggers appeared, removed their caps and stuffed them into the apron of their overalls. The four men hoisted the simple wooden coffin onto their shoulders.

What followed was the fastest burial Marcus had ever witnessed. The bearers put down their burden at the side of the grave, took hold of the ropes and had the coffin lowered in a trice. No officiant appeared to utter prayers over Fred Chadwick as he was assigned to his eternal rest. Deschanel supported Maggie with an arm around her waist. Not one of the mourners shed a tear. In fact, most of the attendees peering into the grave seemed intent on making sure Chadwick was well and truly buried.

The silence was broken only by the sound of baby birds demanding to be fed. A lone crow cawed in the distance.

Marcus hoped there would be people to mourn him when he died. Eliza was gone, her lungs destroyed by cotton dust in the factory where she'd worked. He'd wept buckets at her funeral in this very cemetery, knowing in his heart he'd never be blessed by another love as deep.

At a nod from Deschanel, the gravediggers began shoveling dirt into the hole.

Grief and loneliness swept over Marcus as bitter memories engulfed him. Should he stop by Eliza's grave—or not?

He struggled to pull himself together when Maggie told the gathering she had an announcement to make if they'd all kindly gather at *The Hippodrome* this afternoon.

MAGGIE THANKED God that Edouard was there to hold her up as Fred's coffin was lowered into the grave. Guilt tightened her throat. She could summon no feelings of sorrow. What kind of woman felt relief that her husband was dead? Only a trollop sought solace in the support of another man.

Years of marriage to an abusive bully had taken their toll. She would never get those lost years back. Fred had destroyed the Maggie she used to be. She was no longer trusting and optimistic.

It was only on stage that she caught occasional glimpses of the old Maggie.

She was drawn to Edouard Deschanel, but could she trust him?

"Rest in peace," she muttered as the coffin squelched into the muddy bottom of the grave.

Glancing around nervously, she wondered if anyone could discern her true thoughts.

I hope you rot in hell, bastard.

As the others drifted away, Goliath took his nervous girlfriend's hand and led her to the edge of the grave. "Take a good look," he told Maria. "He won't bother you again."

She looked up at him with those big, blue eyes that never failed to please him. "Who do you think killed him?" she asked. "It must have taken strength."

"Whoever it was did us all a favor," he replied, worried she suspected perhaps he was the murderer. After all, he was the theater's strongman.

"Not if *The Hippodrome* closes and we're all unemployed."

As they followed the rest of the mourners out of the cemetery, he realized he hadn't thought of that possibility.

Back at the theater, Maggie felt safe as she clung to Edouard in the privacy behind the heavy stage curtains, but uncertainty lay like a lead ball in her belly. "I can't shake off this feeling of guilt," she admitted. "I couldn't cry at the cemetery. All I felt was relief."

"That's your husband's fault, not yours," Edouard replied, taking her into his arms. "He killed whatever love you once felt for him."

"I often wished to be free of his brutality," she confessed, melting into his strength. "But I never wished for his death."

Someone had killed Fred in a violent manner that spoke of hatred and anger. "I wish I knew the murderer's identity," she murmured, longing for a drink.

"As do I," he replied. "Until they are caught, you and I will be under suspicion."

"Then we must do what we can to find out who killed Fred."

"No, *chérie*, not *we*. I will investigate. It could be dangerous and you are to stay out of it."

"Some people will be offended," she said. "But I think reopening the theater and carrying on with the performances is a good idea, don't you?"

They broke apart when they heard voices in the main hall.

"If one of the theater's employees is guilty," he whispered, "it's good they remain here where we can keep an eye on them, but I fear for your safety."

"You will make sure I'm safe," she whispered, confident that, at last, she had a champion to watch over her. "For all we know, the killer could be someone from outside. Fred thought I wasn't aware of the opium den in the cellar, but punters who've had a drink too many tend to run off at the mouth."

"Opium den?" Edouard exclaimed.

"Dog fights too, I understand. And cock fighting."

"*Mon Dieu!*" he exclaimed. "Such enterprises involve dangerous people. Do the police know about this?"

"I did mention it, but they may not have believed me."

As agreed, Edouard stayed behind the curtain while she found her way off the stage and into the hall. Already feeling the need for a drink without his support, she planned to announce to the employees that the theater would reopen and performances continue for the time being. Anyone who seemed unhappy with her decision might be the killer, although almost everyone would censure her for not observing a year of mourning.

Sitting at a table on the main floor of the music hall, Marcus instructed Walsh to keep an eye on the strongman. "Mrs. Chadwick's either going to announce the closure of *The Hippodrome*, or she plans to keep the place going."

"She can't perform if we arrest her," Walsh replied.

Marcus sighed. "Just monitor Goliath, or whatever his real name is. He'd have the strength to garrote another man."

"But why would he kill his employer?"

"Perhaps you haven't noticed his attachment to the little cigarette girl?"

"And you think ..."

Marcus pressed a finger to his lips when Mrs. Chadwick appeared onstage. "Thank you all for coming," she began, clearing her throat when her voice faltered.

Marcus found it fascinating that a seasoned performer famous for her stage presence seemed nervous in front of a group of people she knew very well. Perhaps she sensed the killer sat among them.

She took a deep breath. "And thank you for attending Fred's burial."

Only the waiter reacted. "Fastest funeral I've ever attended," he quipped.

Everyone else nodded, but stern faces indicated no one found the remark amusing. Marcus wondered why the waiter seemed nervous.

"I've decided to keep *The Hippodrome* going," Mrs. Chadwick declared. When the cheering died down, she continued. "I'll depend on all of you to do your best to help our beloved theater recover from this horror. The show must go on. People depend on us to brighten their hard lives. We'll reopen this very night."

"Hear, hear," resounded.

Only the cigarette girl remained quiet.

Marcus was preoccupied with pondering what this development might mean when Walsh announced, "Inspector Halliwell would like to speak to each of you, just to ascertain if you saw or heard anything unusual the night of the murder."

Perhaps the young constable had the makings of a competent policeman after all.

Chapter 9

Things Are Not What They Seem

Marcus decided to begin his questioning with the cigarette girl. Mrs. Chadwick had suggested he conduct the interviews onstage. The heavy velvet curtains would provide privacy. Goliath and the waiter carried a table and chairs up from the main floor of the hall. The cigarette girl fidgeted nervously with the sleeve of her coat and avoided looking at Goliath. The strongman glared at Marcus, confirming what he suspected. Goliath and the cigarette girl were an item.

Walsh stood behind the table, notebook and pencil at the ready.

"No need to be nervous," Marcus said. "Please state your full name."

"Maria Lonsdale," she replied as she sat, her gaze fixed on the table.

"And how long have you worked at *The Hippodrome?*"

"A few months."

"Do you like working here?"

"Mostly," she replied shyly after some hesitation. "The tips are good."

Given her attractive face and youthful curves, Marcus could well imagine Maria often had to fight off some of the punters. And perhaps Fred Chadwick.

"Do you get along with the other people here?"

"Most of them."

"I notice Goliath seems to care for you."

She glanced up then quickly averted her eyes again. "Yes, he's my boyfriend, but he'd never do anything to harm Mr. Chadwick, even if he was angry."

"Why would he be angry with his employer?"

Maria squirmed. "I don't like to speak ill of the dead, but Mr. Chadwick took liberties."

Marcus' suspicions were correct. "And that annoyed Goliath."

"Mr. Chadwick left me alone when Goliath was around."

"He was afraid of the theater's strongman."

She glanced up again, her eyes full of panic. "Yes. But Goliath is gentle. He would never murder anyone."

"Thank you, Miss Lonsdale. That's all for now."

After she left the stage, Marcus turned to Walsh. "Well?"

"She thinks her boyfriend is guilty."

"I agree. Let's question him next."

RESTLESS AND UNEASY after Maggie's suggestion an opium den was operating beneath *The Hippodrome*, Edouard left the theater during her announcement. He reasoned it would take but a few minutes to reconnoiter outside in order to find an entry into the cellar. He wandered into the narrow, cobblestone alley that ran alongside the building, startled when a dark-skinned fellow emerged from a doorway that Edouard hadn't noticed. The well-dressed foreigner looked more like a prosperous businessman than a criminal and he seemed as taken aback by the encounter as Edouard.

"Lookin' fer sumat?" the scowling man asked with a broad Lancashire accent.

So, not a foreigner.

"Just exploring," Edouard replied, exaggerating his French accent. "I'm new to the town."

"Tha'd best be careful wandrin' down back alleys."

"*Merci*, I appreciate the advice," he replied before walking hastily back to the street.

He returned to the hall in time to see the flustered cigarette girl fight her way out from behind the stage curtain. Maggie hurried to console the weeping girl. Edouard held up a finger. "One minute," he promised, regretting the disappointment on her face.

The constable appeared and called for Goliath, the strongman. Assuming the police were conducting interviews behind the curtains, Edouard approached the young policeman. "Could I have a word with the inspector?" he asked. "I have new information which might prove useful."

Ushered onto the stage, Edouard wasted no time. "Mrs. Chadwick has informed me a criminal enterprise has been operating in the cellar below the hall."

"An opium den, I believe," Halliwell replied with a nod.

Deflated, Edouard slumped into a vacant chair. "You already know."

"We've investigated and found only an Indian gentleman purporting to store flags and bunting in the space."

"I just met him," Edouard said with a smile. "I was surprised to hear a dark-skinned man speak with a strong Lancashire accent."

Halliwell frowned. "Short, dapper chap, dressed in black business attire. Top hat."

"*Oui*."

"And he didn't speak with an Indian accent?"

"Definitely not."

"Thank you, Mr. Deschanel. That's most informative."

MAGGIE WAS RELIEVED to see Edouard reenter the hall. Without him by her side, she felt weak and in need of a drink. She was past the point of caring who saw them when he hurried to join her and took hold of her hands.

"I told the inspector about the opium den," he explained.

"What did he say?"

"They've been down there to investigate, but I get the feeling the inspector thinks—how do you say—things are not what they seem."

"I would guess the criminals covered their tracks quickly with all the policemen around."

"I ventured down the alley to see if I could find out anything useful."

Her heart lurched. "Please be careful."

"Nothing untoward happened, except I bumped into an Indian chap coming out of a door to the cellar. Oddly enough, he looked foreign but spoke with a Lancashire accent."

She shivered. "That would be Rajendra Bandi. He used to come into the hall occasionally to see my husband. I suspected he and Fred were in cahoots, though they weren't friendly toward one another. He met with Fred in the office and never stayed to watch the show. Gave me the creeps."

"I think the inspector suspects him of being involved in criminal activities. Hopefully, he'll keep after the fellow."

Her throat tightened. "I wouldn't be surprised if he turns out to be the killer."

After questioning Goliath, whose real name turned out to be Joe Peel, Marcus was more undecided than ever. Peel's impressive muscles left no doubt he had the strength to strangle a man with his bare hands, but therein lay a quandary. Why would a simple farm lad from Blackrod choose a garrote?

Maria might wrongly suspect her boyfriend had murdered Chadwick, but she was right about one thing. Joe Peel was a gentle soul who seemed incapable of telling lies. When asked about Chadwick, he readily confessed to hating the man. "'E treated me like I were nowt and couldn't keep 'is grubby 'ands off me girl."

"Did you hate him enough to kill him?" Walsh asked.

"Wish I'd 'ad the courage," the lad admitted. "And I'm nay sorry 'e's dead, though it puts Maggie in a bind."

"How so?"

"Well, only time will tell if the punters end up avoiding this place. We might all be out of a job soon."

"What will you do then?"

Joe gave the matter some thought. "I could take Maria 'ome to me mum and dad's farm, but 'er family depends on the wage she earns 'ere."

"He's either a very good liar," Walsh observed after Peel left. "Or he's innocent."

"The latter, I believe," Marcus replied, pleased with his constable's thoughtful analysis. "None of the performers stand to gain from Chadwick's death and they could lose their livelihoods. I think we should investigate Mr. Bandi's cellar more thoroughly. You know the old saying—*there's no honor among thieves."*

RAJENDRA TOOK off his top hat and threw it aside. He hated what the confounded thing did to his glossy black hair, but needs must when a man is playing a part. Contemplating the boxes of useless merchandise, he startled when someone rapped on the cellar door. His men had spread the word that the cock fights wouldn't resume for at least another week, so it could only be the police at the door.

He settled the hat back on his head and hurried to turn the key in the lock. "Inspector," he declared, bowing low. "Namaste. To what do I owe the pleasure?"

Halliwell pushed past him. "For starters, you can drop the phony accent."

"I'm sure I don't know what you mean," he replied, bowing politely.

"Give it a rest, Bandi," the constable hissed as he followed his superior into the cellar. "You've never set foot in India, so why the pretense?"

Rajendra realized more lies would simply make the pair more suspicious. "Tha's caught me owt," he confessed. "I's just a Bolton lad tryin' to meck a livin'."

"Doing what?" Halliwell asked, eyeing the boards nailed over the door of the opium den. "And don't tell me you sell musty flags and bunting."

Frantically searching his mind for a plausible explanation for the boards, Rajendra froze when the nosy constable picked up a foot long piece of wire. "Sir," the policeman called, holding up his find.

"Well, well," the inspector said as he took the wire from his constable. "How do you explain this?"

The wire was from one of the hay bales that formed the walls of the dog-fighting pit, but Rajendra could hardly reveal that. "It's a piece of wire," he said with a shrug.

"Perhaps the one used to garrote Mr. Chadwick," Halliwell replied. "I'm placing you under arrest for his murder, Mr. Bandi."

Chapter 10

We Need More Evidence

A fragile optimism told hold in Maggie's heart. "Everyone is working hard to get the place ready for tonight," she told Edouard. "We can only hope the patrons come back."

"I've posted notices on the windows of *Shangri-La,*" he replied. "My customers might not be your regular clientele, but passersby on Deansgate will see them."

"Only time will tell," she murmured, aware some of Edouard's patrons would disapprove of his support.

"They miss their Music Hall Queen," he assured her, taking her into his embrace. "They'll be back in droves."

She tensed when Inspector Halliwell and his constable strode into the hall, but Edouard refused to let her pull away. "We have no reason to feel guilty," he whispered.

"Good news," Halliwell shouted, attracting everyone's attention. "We've made an arrest."

Winged creatures fluttered in Maggie's insides as excited employees and performers gathered around the policemen.

"Who is it?" Edouard asked.

Halliwell pointed to a wire in his constable's hands. "We found this down in the cellar, so we've arrested Mr. Bandi."

One eyebrow raised, Edouard reached for the wire. "You believe he garroted Chadwick with this?" he asked when Walsh handed over the evidence.

Halliwell frowned. "You sound skeptical."

"It's too short and there's no blood on it as far as I can see."

"Bandi could have wiped it off," the constable suggested.

"If that's the case, would he carelessly leave it lying about for us to find?" Halliwell asked, sounding too doubtful for Maggie's liking. If Bandi wasn't guilty, a violent killer was still on the loose.

"WE NEED MORE EVIDENCE," Marcus declared reluctantly. "Back to the cellar." He'd been sure Bandi was guilty and his disappointment was reflected in Walsh's eyes. However, Deschanel was right. The wire was much too short to use as a garrote.

"Perhaps I may accompany you," the shopkeeper said. "Another pair of eyes on the place, so to speak."

Marcus doubted the Frenchman had any connection to Bandi, so he agreed. If Deschanel were the killer, he might hang himself if given enough rope.

The three men exited the hall and located the door in the alley. The policeman posted to guard the entrance opened it for them and they stepped inside.

Deschanel inhaled. "Opium," he said without hesitation. "But what has Bandi done with the addicts?"

"No reports of any corpses on the streets," Walsh replied.

"If he didn't move them to another building, the wretches must still be here somewhere," Marcus concluded.

They spread out to search the large cellar. Deschanel found bits of straw around the piles of boxes. "Might explain the wire," he suggested. "Bales of hay, perhaps used to construct the perimeter for dog fighting."

"You seem to know a lot about this kind of thing," Marcus replied.

"Maggie mentioned dog and cock fights, and a man cannot frequent the streets of Paris without becoming aware how such things operate."

Walsh and Marcus exchanged a doubtful glance before continuing to search the shadows of the dank cellar. They found nothing until Marcus noticed the rough boards nailed to one wall. "I thought this seemed odd before," he muttered. "Walsh, send the constable in the alley to fetch a crowbar."

Sᴉᴄᴋᴇɴᴇᴅ by what he and the policemen discovered in the cellar when the boards were removed and the hidden door forced open, Edouard returned to the hall. As if Maggie didn't have enough to worry about, now he'd have to tell her about the human detritus they'd found beneath her beloved theater.

He took a seat beside Maria at a table and watched as Maggie worked with Goliath on his routine, apparently suggesting changes. It was a savvy move in Edouard's opinion. The punters who returned this first night would tell their friends and neighbors about improvements to the acts.

He and Maria applauded enthusiastically when Goliath took his final bow and exited the stage.

Edouard rose to kiss Maggie on both cheeks when she came to sit with them. "Did you find anything?" she asked.

"Not to do with the murder," he confessed. "However, I think Mr. Bandi will be in jail a long time."

"Don't tell me," she said with a shudder. "I've heard about the horrors of opium dens."

"Before we get to that, I must congratulate you on making changes to the performances. It's a good idea."

"Everyone seems to think so, except the new comedian. He insists on sticking to his repertoire."

"*Tant pis*," Edouard replied. "Too bad. His jokes are *ringardes—corn*, I think you say."

"Corny. I agree. I don't know what Fred saw in him. He has no personality."

"You're right, Mrs. Chadwick," the waiter declared as he joined them. "I told Fred that hiring him was a mistake."

"You're braver than most, Emerson," Maggie replied with a smile. "I'll wager he didn't take the criticism well."

"No, but I was used to that. He never listened to me. At least I didn't end up with his fist in my face like you, *Monsieur*."

"You have a good feel for my language," Edouard replied, genuinely impressed with the waiter's pronunciation. "Do you speak French?"

"*Oui. Un peu. J'ai travaillé dans un restaurant à Calais pendant quelques mois.*"

Edouard translated for Maggie. "Did you know Emerson worked in a restaurant in Calais for a few months?"

"No, I didn't," she replied.

"Probably because I didn't tell Fred," Emerson confessed.

As the conversation continued, Edouard wondered why the waiter hadn't revealed experience that would encourage an employer to hire him. What other secrets was he harboring?

EMERSON CHUCKLED. The Frenchman was no doubt wondering why he hadn't told Fred about his experience working abroad. The answer was simple. When he'd applied in response to the advertisement about the job, Emerson had quickly realized Fred Chadwick wasn't interested in his past. Nor was he the kind of man to whom you divulged personal information. He'd for sure find a way to use it against you.

IT TOOK all day for Marcus and Walsh to transport the half dozen lost souls from the opium den to the new workhouse outside of town in Farnworth. Before they could even set out, procuring a wagon gobbled up precious time. Marcus wasn't confident the workhouse was the place to lodge the addicts, but, as the Superintendent pointed out, there seemed to be no alternative. Bandi had been locked up in the cells, but the nick was no place for human wreckage. Most of the addicts couldn't even walk, or talk coherently. They didn't seem aware of what was happening, except for the mournful wailing and belligerence when the effects of the drug began to wear off.

"Police work can sometimes be challenging," he told Walsh who looked like he might retch over the side of the wagon as the miles dragged by.

His mouth set in a stern line, the constable merely nodded.

It was the first time Marcus had seen the impressive new Fishpool workhouse, opened just the previous year. Dominated by a central tower, the three-story building was like something transported from Italy. It was a far cry from the old workhouse in the town center on Fletcher Street.

The master and matron were not pleased to welcome the new inmates. "This is a strictly run establishment," the sour-faced matron informed Marcus. "We operate on the principles of economy and discipline."

The master gave instructions to a porter. The newcomers were to be stripped and washed, then given fresh clothing. The garments in which they'd arrived were to be burned.

Marcus understood the directive. It was likely the skeletal men had worn the same tattered clothes for months.

"They'll all be dead within the week," Walsh observed as they left the premises.

Sadly, Marcus agreed with him. He had no experience dealing with people addicted to opium, but suspected economy and discipline weren't what the wretches needed. "The same fate awaited them if we'd left them in the cellar," he replied.

Chapter 11

New Memories

Nervous anticipation had tied Maggie's innards in knots. If the patrons didn't come back, she'd have to close the theater. Peeking through the curtains, she realized she needn't have worried. The hall had filled up quickly with a chattering crowd of people obviously excited to be back in their favorite music hall.

Buoyed by the large number of patrons who'd returned, and satisfied she'd warmed them up with her usual repertoire, Maggie made an announcement. "In honor of our reopening, we have a new song for you, written by our own orchestra conductor."

Beaming with pride, Morris took a bow, even his bald head blushing. She hadn't been aware that the musician had often suggested new music but Fred wouldn't even listen. Confident the punters would love it, she'd agreed to incorporate the song as soon as she read the lyrics.

"So, here we go," she proclaimed as the orchestra played the opening bars.

In the early light of morning,

Anna Markland

> *When the whistle sounds its call,*
> *We rise to face the dawning,*
> *In the cotton mills so tall.*
> *Our hands are rough and weary,*
> *From the looms we tend each day,*
> *But with hearts unbowed and cheery,*
> *We forge our humble way.*

She led them through the first chorus line by line.

> *Oh, the toil of the mill worker,*
> *With sweat 'pon our brow,*
> *We spin threads for others,*
> *Because we know how.*
> *Strength and grit will guide us,*
> *Through the darkest, longest night,*
> *For together we are mighty*
> *And together we shall fight.*

Glad to hear applause, she began the second verse.

> *In the rows beneath the roof,*
> *Where the machines never rest,*
> *We dream of brighter futures,*
> *And a life that's truly blessed.*
> *Though the wages be meager,*
> *And the days long and hard,*
> *We carry on with vigor,*
> *Fueled by dreams we guard.*

As she expected, the gallery joined her in the chorus. The whistling, boot stomping and loud applause assured her and the furiously sweating conductor that the audience loved the new song.

~

EMERSON DIDN'T CARE that he was neglecting his duties. He couldn't take his eyes off Maggie. She held him and the audience spellbound.

She claimed the conductor had written the new song, but Emerson doubted Morris Ince had it in him. The lyrics had come from her kind heart.

The only fly in the ointment was the presence of the Frenchman. Emerson had to think of a way to get him out of the picture.

~

LEAPING TO HIS FEET, Edouard applauded and cheered louder than anyone when Maggie took her final bow. As he'd predicted, patrons had flocked in droves to the reopening of *The Hippodrome*. While some might fault her performing when she was expected to be in mourning, no one could criticize the artful changes made to her costume by the local seamstress who did occasional work for the hall. The added layers of black crepe were a respectful touch and the punters appreciated her effort to honor a man who was universally disliked.

The audience had raised its collective voice to the rafters and joined Maggie in singing the songs they loved and the conductor's piece. They repeated her new joke over and over to each other, even after she'd left the stage and the dancers hurried in from the wings to end the show.

The cheering audience immediately recognized the opening bars of the can-can music, but Edouard doubted they knew it had been composed by Offenbach. The composer was likely delighted that his *Galop Infernal* was still prompting patrons to cheer wildly when female dancers in crotchless pantalets high-kicked their way across the stage.

A slightly tipsy Foster apparently felt the need to lean over to Edouard and repeat Maggie's new one-liner. "What did the horse say after it tripped?"

"I don't know," he replied, deciding it was easier to play along.

"I've fallen and I can't giddy-up. Hah! Do you get it?"

"Yes, I get it," he replied, thrilled for Maggie's success. It seemed the ordinary folk of Bolton were happy to see the back of Fred Chadwick and more than glad to return to the music hall.

Intending to go to Maggie's dressing room, Edouard rose from his seat.

"Don't you want to see Goliath's act?" Foster asked. "Rumor has it he's changed a few things."

"He has, and you'll enjoy it," he assured his store manager.

While the dancers were taking their bow and blowing kisses to the whistling crowd in the gallery, he strode purposefully down the corridor. He'd often heard it said that music halls provided a vital respite from the backbreaking tedium of long hours in the mills, but he'd never really understood before. The wretched addicts used opium to escape life's realities. Lancashire's working men and women craved the laughter and joy to be found in the music hall.

"It's Edouard," he said softly as he tapped on the dressing room door.

~

EDOUARD'S VOICE REASSURED MAGGIE. She had to stop flinching every time someone tapped on her door. "Come in," she said, rising to greet him when he entered.

"You were wonderful," he exclaimed, taking her into his arms. "*Merveilleuse.*"

"It was easier to perform knowing you were watching me and not Fred," she admitted. "Now, if I could just exorcise him from this room."

"We could share a kiss," he suggested. "That way you'll think of your dressing room as the place where we kissed for the first time."

Suddenly seized by an urge to stretch and purr like a cat, Maggie closed her eyes and sighed.

"I'll take that as permission," he said.

Maggie had been married for too many years, but Fred had never nibbled her lips. Edouard teased and coaxed, then gently delved his tongue into her eager mouth. Soon, his hips echoed the rhythm of his tongue's explorations as he tightened his embrace. Intoxicated by his subtle cologne, Maggie felt the unmistakable strength of his desire pressed against her. Thankful she'd decided against drinking a tot of gin before performing, she trembled with a need to surrender to this beautiful man.

Even at the beginning of Fred's courtship, Maggie had always been afraid of his unpredictable temper. She'd known Edouard only a few days, yet sensed she could trust him with her body and her heart. She sifted her fingers into the silky hair at his nape, unable to deny the wanton feelings coursing through her body. "Let's go to my flat," she whispered when he ended the kiss, instantly regretting the impulse to invite him into Fred's dingy lair.

~

Edouard agreed to accompany Maggie to her flat, but had no intention of making love to her there. They left by the theater's back entrance. As he escorted her along Churchgate to Bank Street, then up the narrow, winding staircase, he pondered his next move. Once inside the cramped space, he took her into his arms and tried to explain. "I want you, Maggie, more than I've ever wanted a woman."

Something in his voice must have alerted her. "But ...," she began, attempting to pull away.

He held fast. "Do not mistake my meaning. It might kill me to walk away from here without making love to you."

He regretted the words as soon as they were out of his mouth. "I apologize. That was an unfortunate turn of phrase."

She rested her head on his chest, the fight apparently gone out of her. "I understand. It's this place."

"Exactly. This is Chadwick's domain. I suspect you suffered more abuse than tender moments here."

He regretted dragging up bitter memories when a ragged sigh escaped her lips. "Come to the store tomorrow afternoon. I keep an *appartement* there. We'll make new memories."

His hopes soared when she looked up at him, her eyes full of longing, and murmured, "Kiss me again."

Emerson Dean leaned back against the cold, stone wall behind *The Hippodrome* and tried to steady his breathing. Taking a much-needed break from serving inebriated punters, he'd come outside for a breath of air.

Recalling Maggie's breathtaking performance tonight, he swallowed the lump in his throat. She'd had the audience in the palm of her hand. They loved her, and he understood. He'd wanted her since his first day working at the theater, but he'd been too afraid of Fred to do anything about it. The brute was finally gone, but the bloody Frenchman had suddenly appeared on the scene and Emerson had just seen the pair leaving by the rear entrance. He closed his eyes and clenched his jaw, then hurried to the front of the theater and watched them turn right onto Bank Street. Arm in arm, they were headed for her flat. Life was so unfair.

As he made his way back into the rowdy hall, he resolved to reveal his feelings to Maggie. Surely she'd see he was a better catch than a French shopkeeper, otherwise he'd waited too long to be free of Fred's abusive disregard and hurtful insults.

Chapter 12

Pomade

"We can't go in there," Walsh declared.

"Why not?" Marcus replied.

"Well, the ladies, they might be, you know, unclothed."

Marcus suddenly realized his young constable had probably never seen a woman in the all-together. "Just keep your eyes on their feet," he advised as they entered the dancers' dressing room after tapping on the door and receiving permission to enter.

The space provided for the troupe of a dozen dancers was no bigger than a cupboard, so the odor of female sweat wasn't altogether unexpected. Three of the women lounged, squeezed together on a old settee designed for two people, breasts overflowing their scanty bodices. They were still out of breath after their performance which only added to the tempting display. Attempting to clean off stage makeup, four more dancers elbowed each other as they vied for a turn at the one cracked mirror.

"What's this?" one of the girls on the settee asked, opening her legs as she looked at Walsh with hooded eyes. "Cum fer a closer look?"

The constable blushed when all the women giggled, but he took out his notebook and did as Marcus had instructed.

"This will only take a minute, ladies," Marcus said. "We simply want to know if you saw anything unusual the night Mr. Chadwick was killed."

"Tha suspects one of us?"

Marcus shook his head. "No, but you may have witnessed something suspicious."

Utter silence and pouts greeted his words, which wasn't what he'd hoped for.

"Chadwick were a monster," one finally blurted out. "We're all glad 'e's dead."

"Aye," chimed the chorus.

"So, nobody saw anything untoward."

"Blimey, that's a big word. No, we didn't, but tha should question that greasy waiter."

Several heads nodded general agreement.

"Emerson Dean?"

"He's allus 'ad a thing for Maggie. Thinks the world of 'er. And 'e'd be one o' the last to leave."

Marcus was tempted to laugh. Maggie Chadwick and the officious little waiter with the ridiculous hairstyle? Never in a million years. However, if Dean's feelings ran deep, he may have been tempted to kill Chadwick. Many men probably lusted after the voluptuous Maggie—which brought his thoughts full circle back to Edouard Deschanel.

"Done for the day, are we, Inspector?" Walsh asked after they left the chorus girls.

"No, not yet. It's nearly closing time. Let's find Emerson Dean."

THE LAST ROWDY patrons were staggering out of the music hall when Emerson sensed the policemen approaching. He was surprised and a little annoyed it had taken them so long to get to him. Was he not important enough to be questioned?

"Emerson Dean?" the inspector asked.

"That's me," he replied, flippantly, adjusting his black armband. The policeman knew full well who he was, so why the formality? "How can I help you?"

The yawning constable gestured to a table. "We have a few questions if you'd like to take a seat for a moment."

"Of course," he replied, setting down his tray full of empty glasses on the table as he sat. "I take it you plan to arrest the frog."

"Why would we do that?" the inspector retorted. "Do you know something we don't?"

Apprehension shivered up Emerson's spine. Had he over-played his hand? "Well, I'm sure you know Mr. Chadwick and the Frenchman had a fight, right here. We all saw it. If Fred had done what I suggested and gone to the infirmary afterward to get his nose seen to, he might still be alive."

Halliwell narrowed his eyes. "We are aware there was a brawl. You think Mr. Deschanel later killed Mr. Chadwick?"

"Well, it's obvious he lusts after Mrs. Chadwick. The two of them are in her flat now, doing who knows what?"

Emerson swallowed hard when the policemen exchanged a knowing glance. He'd said too much.

"Are you jealous of the Frenchman?" the Inspector asked.

Emerson should admit he had been enamored of Maggie forever, but that might land him in trouble. "Why would I be jealous?" he exclaimed.

"Well, he's a successful businessman who seems to have attracted Mrs. Chadwick's eye, whereas you ..."

Emerson bristled when the Inspector eyed his hair—yet

another Neanderthal who understood nothing about fashion. "I'm quite content with my lot in life," he lied.

"Serving all these patrons must be hard for one person," Walsh said.

"Sally Fry comes in to help on Fridays and Saturdays," Emerson replied, "Though I don't consider Sally to be much help. Too busy flaunting her endowments to the punters, if you get my drift."

"Does she serve in the gallery?" Walsh asked.

Tempted to scoff at the policeman's naiveté, he replied, "We don't serve those people. They can't afford our prices and usually bring their own tipple anyway. Will there be anything else?"

"That's all for now. We may need to speak to you again."

❧

"Doubtful," Marcus said in response to his constable's inquiring look. "Did you see the greasy finger marks on the empty glasses? If Dean tried to hold a wire, it would slip right through his pomaded fingers!"

It was the first time he'd seen Walsh crack a smile.

"His pomade is heavily perfumed but we didn't detect even a faint trace on the body. Besides, I can't see him overpowering Fred Chadwick. He's too small, and Fred was no weakling."

"Sometimes, hatred gives men strength they didn't know they had," Walsh replied.

Marcus nodded, wondering where his reportedly inexperienced constable had learned that truth. "So, let's recap. We can rule out the chorus girls. They're a pack. If one of them had broken ranks, they'd snitch."

"And I didn't notice any attempt to remove bloodstains from any of the costumes," Walsh added.

Marcus was impressed. His constable was learning to look for clues. "Good point. Same goes for Maria Lonsdale and her strongman boyfriend. They don't have it in them to garrote a man."

"I agree, sir."

Marcus scratched his scalp. "That leaves us with the rest of the performers, the Frenchman, and Maggie herself."

"We've already established it's unlikely a woman alone couldn't have done it."

Much as he didn't want to admit it, they were running out of suspects. "Unless she had the Frenchman's help."

Chapter 13

Shopping

The next morning, Maggie hardly recognized the woman who gazed back from the mirror. Kissed so thoroughly by Edouard before he'd left the previous evening, she'd barely slept, preoccupied and excited by the invitation to his apartment. Yet, her reflection showed a smiling woman whose bright eyes spoke of the promise of intimacy with an attractive man she was growing very fond of. She hadn't even thought about having a fortifying drink.

She completed her toilette, deciding against using the cheap perfume Fred had given her as a token of his regret after one particularly nasty beating. She tried on several outfits, but eventually settled on her mourning clothes in deference to societal expectations. She donned her black coat and tied the black shot silk ties of a close fitting straw bonnet trimmed with white lace beneath her chin. The gossips would have to be satisfied with that.

Her black boots were sturdy, though not the height of fashion. She might buy a new pair at *Shangri-La*. Perhaps Edouard would be willing to extend credit.

With one last reassuring perusal of her appearance in the

mirror, she set off, climbing the Bank Street hill and turning right onto Deansgate.

She'd long since become accustomed to people recognizing her on the streets of the town center. They usually fell into two groups. Working class men and women greeted her with an enthusiastic smile and a cheery hello. The few gentry who were out and about without a carriage turned away as if from a bad smell.

This day, no one met her gaze. Whispers of *murder* and loud tutting sounds replaced polite greetings. Head held high, she walked on, carefully sidestepping potholes and piles of rubbish. She stopped only once to peek at the tempting meringues and sponge cakes on display in Laidlaw's window. Let folk censure her. She and Edouard were innocent and had an exciting afternoon ahead of them.

She faltered when a carriage pulled up alongside. Alarm fled when she recognized it from the funeral as Edouard's. The darling man had sent his carriage for her.

The driver hailed her as he came around to let down the steps. "Sorry, Mrs. Chadwick. I were s'posed to arrive at thy flat before tha left."

Pausing to look around and make sure she had an audience, she lifted the hem of her skirt and accepted Albert's hand to board the elegant carriage.

It took only a minute for the driver to turn the carriage around in the busy street then they were proceeding at a clip along Deansgate. Edouard was waiting outside *Shangri-La* to help her alight. He'd called her the Music Hall Queen. She felt like royalty as he kissed her hand, his green eyes full of mischief.

~

Edouard couldn't believe his luck. The shipment from the House of Worth in Paris had arrived this very morning. Miss Horrocks and her ladies were still unpacking, but Edouard couldn't wait to show the gowns to Maggie.

She gasped when he escorted her up to the Ladies' Wear department on the second floor and she saw one of the gowns already on display.

"Newly arrived from Paris," he explained.

Miss Horrocks pursed her thin lips when Maggie reached to finger the shimmering taffeta of a light gray receiving gown. "It's so simple, yet so elegant," she whispered.

He ought to have known Maggie would quickly recognize the genius of Charles Frederick Worth. He'd sensed she would enjoy seeing the exclusive fashions, but suddenly he wanted to gift the gown to her. "Why not try it on?" he suggested.

She stepped back abruptly, but the gleam in her eyes belied her reluctance. "I couldn't possibly afford ..."

"You need something suitable for mourning," he replied. "It's not black, but you can always silence critics by telling them it's the custom for widows to wear gray in Paris."

"You are naughty," she said, her eyes sparkling. "But ..."

"You think that was naughty. Wait until we get to my *appartement*."

"Edouard," she whispered shyly, as he helped her remove her coat, smugly pleased his teasing had managed to make her pebbled nipples poke at the fabric of her blouse.

"Miss Horrocks," he called. "Please set up an account for Madame Chadwick and prepare a dressing room with this gown."

"I will personally guarantee the account," he added when the scowling matron huffed and puffed.

"She doesn't approve of me," Maggie said softly when Miss Horrocks left to search for an assistant.

"Do you care?" he asked, leaning close to her ear. "I approve of you and that's all that counts in *Shangri-La*."

~

ON OCCASION, one of the chorus girls assisted Maggie with her costume and make-up for a performance. More often than not, she dressed herself, as she did with her everyday clothes. Reliant on *The Hippodrome's* part-time seamstress for the tailoring of her garments—even her unmentionables—it had been years since she'd purchased any item of clothing from a store. Though she was the star attraction at the theater, Fred gave her only a pittance as her allowance. She had no idea how much money the music hall brought in. He kept the takings locked in his office to which she had no access. From the meager sum he gave her, she was expected to pay rent for the flat and provide food for the two of them—not that Fred ate many of his meals at home and she'd be the first to admit she was a mediocre cook. It used to be of some consolation that he bought his own expensively tailored outfits.

When the sour-faced Miss Horrocks informed Edouard the dressing room was ready, Maggie hesitated. "I'm not sure about this," she began.

Edouard nodded. "Remiss of me," he replied, taking her arm. "I should have considered you'd like to try new lingerie with the gown."

Heat flooded Maggie's face when he escorted her to a display of silk underthings. "Oh, my," she gasped.

"Please show Mrs. Chadwick the new stock from Paris," Edouard told the girl serving at the counter.

"Of course, Mr. Deschanel," the smiling young woman replied, ignoring Miss Horrocks' censuring snort. From a bank of glass-fronted drawers located behind her, she pulled out a silk chemise, a pair of crotchless silk pantalets and an embroidered ivory corselet trimmed with ribbons. "I couldn't possibly," Maggie murmured, fingering the exquisite material of the chemise.

Edouard leaned close to her ear. "And I was so looking forward to removing them from your lovely body," he whispered.

Maggie was completely out of her depth with this sophisticated man, but she couldn't resist the temptation to try on undergarments of a quality she hadn't even known existed. When she nodded, the still smiling clerk gathered up the items, and bade Maggie follow her to the dressing room.

IMPATIENT TO SEE Maggie in her new finery, Edouard paced the floor of the Ladies' Wear department. Pretending not to hear the giggles of the salesgirls as he feigned interest in the displays, it came to him he'd been too clever for his own good.

Barging into the private dressing room wasn't an option, no matter how badly he wanted to see Maggie in the silk lingerie. She'd blushed when he teased her about what he had in mind for their tryst, but he was confident she liked being teased. However, an aching arousal had been the penalty.

He tried to analyze his feelings for Maggie. He'd admired her talent as a performer, but, having got to know her a little better, his infatuation intrigued him. She wasn't like any of the women he'd known before—certainly nothing like his faithless wife.

She may not have loved Fred Chadwick, but his murder was gruesome enough to test anyone's mettle. Despite the abuse she'd suffered and the horror of the killing, she'd kept her sense of humor and positive outlook on life. She was hardy and tough, a trait he'd noted in many of the Lancashire folk he'd met. Yet, she was soft and feminine, and very tempting. Only one thing made him hesitate, though he hadn't detected the odor of gin today. After all, who could blame an abused woman for turning to spirits for solace? His mother had done the same. "*Que Dieu accorde son âme,*" he whispered, making the sign of his Savior across his body. "May God rest her soul."

He enjoyed spoiling Maggie with provocative underthings, though he had to admit his motives weren't entirely unselfish.

After they were done here, he'd take her to the jewelry counter and purchase a small bauble for her. Ear-bobs, perhaps.

All thoughts of delaying the tryst in his apartment fled when Maggie stepped out of the dressing room looking like she'd walked off the pages of Worth's catalogue.

Felicity Horrocks fumed. What on earth was Mr. Deschanel thinking? Although, what might one expect from a Frenchman? Perhaps the gown and the glint in his eyes were simply a means to get the music hall trollop into his bed. Hence the lingerie. What a waste! Felicity hadn't accepted the envious position as head of Ladies' Wear to wait on such riffraff.

The harlot was out shopping and flirting with another man when she ought to be in deep mourning—well! The whole affair was offensive and bound to sully the reputation of *Shangri-La*.

Chapter 14

The Apartment

The look in Edouard's eyes when Maggie exited the dressing room was entirely different from the way he'd looked at her when she emerged from the carriage. There was the same admiration, but something else shone in those dark orbs—dare she hope it was love? "Do you like it?" she asked, fluttering her eyelashes. Evidently, decadent undergarments and a fabulous gown turned a woman into a flirt. She was old enough to know better, but still it felt good.

"Like it!" he exclaimed. "You're a vision. The gray compliments your glorious chestnut hair. And the fit—perfect, as I knew it would be."

"I will pay you back, Edouard," she whispered, lest Miss Horrocks be lurking nearby.

He frowned, clearly offended, but said nothing as he offered his arm.

"My coat," she reminded him.

"It will be safe here," he replied. "Lunch is being served—in my apartment. Shall we?"

She accepted his offer of escort, emboldened by the strength of his arm. "We shall," she teased.

Heart beating wildly, she accompanied him to a door that led to an area full of boxes and crates. The workers unpacking them nodded respectfully. "We bring the boxes up on a pulley system," he explained. "That way we can unpack them on the right floor."

"Good idea," she replied, though her mind wasn't on boxes. She was beginning to have doubts about this adventure. Edouard was a sophisticated Frenchman—perhaps too sophisticated for the likes of her.

"My *appartement* is on this floor," he said, turning the handle of a discreet door. "I find it more convenient to live on the premises."

Maggie expected to walk directly into a small flat. Instead, she entered a bright foyer with light blue walls. Nervous, she bent to inhale the fragrance of fresh flowers arranged in a porcelain vase perched atop an elegant wooden console table. "Delightful," she whispered.

"Welcome," he said as he ushered her into the spacious living room. "I hope you'll feel at home."

To her surprise, he sounded nervous. He wanted her good opinion.

Intricate carvings adorned the wooden arms of the furniture. Soft, plush cushions looked invitingly comfortable.

"A fireplace," she exclaimed, wandering over to the ornately carved mantel. Above it, a gilded mirror captured natural light from enormous windows. Landscape paintings adorned the walls. Pale blue floor-to-ceiling draperies framed the windows.

Conscious of his eyes on her, she said, "I feel as though I've entered a foreign country."

"I was born in a small, rural village in Provence," he replied. "I wanted this place to feel like the French countryside."

"You've succeeded, though it feels too elegant to be a simple, country dwelling."

"That's because I'm no longer the simple, country boy I used to be," he growled, coming so close they were nose to nose. Expecting a kiss, she stared at his lips, but he surprised her again. "Let's see what's waiting for us in the dining room," he said with a wink.

"Of course," she replied, surprisingly willing to play the game of heightened anticipation with him.

~

EDOUARD WAS UNCHARACTERISTICALLY NERVOUS. Maggie was the only woman he'd invited into his home—the first place he'd ever had the opportunity to decorate to his own taste. It was important to him she feel comfortable. His cock, in full salute since she'd walked out of the dressing room, urged him to whisk her into the bedroom. However, he sensed her nervousness. He had to be careful not to make her feel she was being seduced by a lascivious Frenchman.

The chef from the store's café had set out their luncheon on the dining room table. The fine china and silverware promised an elegant, intimate lunch. They sat down to eat. She kept admiring the big table and high-backed chairs, exclaiming about the upholstered seats.

She was understandably nervous, and he was reluctant to tell her he rarely sat at the ostentatious table. His apartment was comfortable, and he was satisfied with the ambience he'd worked hard to achieve. However, it struck him full force that his apartment lacked a woman's touch.

The food was simple, but Maggie clearly relished the thick slices of ham and the bread baked in *Shangri-La's* ovens. She confessed she'd never tasted Camembert before and couldn't heap enough praise on its creamy texture. "Your French cheeses are so different from English cheese," she kept saying.

When he raised his glass of white wine and proposed a toast to her health, she studied her glass. "Something wrong?" he asked.

"You probably realized I got tipsy with the wine we drank at luncheon the other day."

"I thought nothing of it," he lied. "You're simply not used to wine."

She avoided meeting his gaze. "You must have been able to tell I'd drunk spirits before that. I have to confess I drink a lot of gin."

He reached for her hand. "Listen, Maggie, I understand. My mother turned to spirits to help her cope with my father's abuse. It infuriated him, though he was the cause."

"Fred was the same. I had to hide the bottles from him."

"I don't want you to feel you have to hide anything from me."

She finally raised her glass. "I want to stop drinking," she said. "In fact, I haven't even thought about having a drink of gin today."

"You won't need alcohol to help you cope anymore," he assured her. "You're safe with me. I wouldn't hurt you for the world." He touched his glass to hers. "Here's to our happiness."

"Happiness," she echoed, though her eyes betrayed her hesitation to believe she could be happy—with him.

He simply had to be patient and give her time to adjust to her new reality. He was certain she'd feel differently after their tryst in the bedroom. But first, he wanted her to feel he was genuinely interested in her as a person. "Have you always lived in Bolton?"

"Born and bred."

"You've seen changes."

"My mother told me this used to be a quiet market town, but

the cotton industry has brought profound changes. Even I have seen more and more factories being built."

"It's now a bustling hub of industrial activity."

"Aye. You can hear the hum of machinery and the rhythmic clatter of looms when you walk down many streets. But it hasn't all been good. Families flocked here from rural areas and other parts of the country. Row upon row of terraced houses were hastily and cheaply built to accommodate them."

"I hear some workers live in appalling conditions."

"That's the reason I sing songs to celebrate them and help them forget the long hours in the mills and the squalor they live in."

"I suppose this cotton famine has hit hard."

"Yes. The mills are the heart of the economy. Without cotton from America, they can't operate, so people have been thrown out of work with no support in many cases."

"You're lucky you don't work in a mill, then."

"Yes. I was blessed with a singing voice and a flair for the stage, thank goodness, though my father didn't approve. He was a spinner and saw nothing wrong with his daughter following in his footsteps. I lasted one day in the mill, but I'll never forget the overwhelming noise of the machines and the blizzard of cotton dust."

Glad to have learned a little more about her, he took her hand when the meal was finished. "It's time," he said softly.

"Yes," she agreed, though she pulled him up short as they passed the small kitchen, apparently enraptured by the copper pots hanging from the railing.

In his mind's eye, he saw Maggie cooking with those pots and serving food to guests at the dining room table. Since his wife's betrayal, he'd avoided commitments with members of the fairer sex—but he wanted Maggie in his life.

Chapter 15

Slowly, Slowly

When Maggie ran out of wonderful things to say about the copper pots, she cast about for something else on which she could heap lavish praise. She chided herself inwardly. It was silly to be nervous. She was a married woman who'd experienced sexual congress before, though she sensed that intimacy with Edouard would be an entirely different experience. However, he was a sophisticated man—French, for goodness sake—and Fred had let her know in no uncertain terms that she was useless in bed.

"Come," he said. "You can explore my kitchen some other time."

"Are you sure about this?" she asked, aware it was a strange question for a woman to ask.

Heat flooded her body when he placed her hand on the substantial bulge in his trousers. "You can see that I am sure. I understand you are nervous but there is no need. I will take precautions."

She couldn't help it—she giggled. The hard flesh beneath her hand was a sure indication Fred had been full of hot air when he'd bragged about the size of his equipment. However,

Edouard's obvious arousal only served to increase her apprehension. Her giggles had probably convinced him she was a brainless ninny. "I'm sorry," she whispered, wishing she knew how to please such a man.

"Come," he said again, leading her by the hand into his bedroom.

She supposed she should comment on the decor, but hardly noticed it, her attention wholly on Edouard as he slowly removed his coat. His cravat followed, then he began to unbutton his shirt.

It hit her like a bolt of lightning that she desperately wanted this beautiful man gazing into her eyes as he disrobed. So, why was she dithering like a virgin? "Let me help you," she said, plucking up her courage as she reached for the buttons with trembling fingers.

SLIDING his arms around Maggie's waist, Edouard acknowledged her decision to help with his buttons as a small victory—the first of many, he hoped.

The fasteners undone, she pushed his shirt off his shoulders and bared his chest. Eyes wide, she sifted her fingers through the light dusting of dark hair.

"Soft," she whispered.

His biceps were imprisoned by the shirt she hadn't fully removed, so he decided to let her explore him. He was already hard, so ...

His cock mocked the wisdom of his reasoning when she brushed her thumbs over his male nipples and licked her lips. Inhaling deeply, he stepped back and freed himself from the shirt. "Let me see you," he said, confident as he tossed the shirt aside that the fear in her eyes had changed to desire.

"It's not a pretty sight," she replied, desire turning to regret in those brown depths.

"Is that what your husband told you?" he asked, turning her gently to give himself access to the fastenings of the gown. He embarked on undoing them when she made no reply. Words wouldn't convince her she was curvaceous and desirable, but worshipping her body might.

She shivered when he eased the unfastened bodice off her shoulders and ran his fingers along the embroidered edge of the corset. Emboldened, he pressed his chest to her back, nuzzled her nape, and reached inside the bodice to lift her breasts free of the corset. As expected, they filled his hands perfectly.

"Edouard," she whispered when he squeezed rigid nipples and nibbled her neck.

He turned her to face him and pulled the bodice down to her waist. Her nipples pouted against the silk chemise which did nothing to hide her bounty. He lowered the straps to reveal her breasts, then leaned forward to swipe his tongue over one nipple, grazing it with his teeth until it hardened.

"Edouard," she breathed, her wide-eyed surprise evident.

The truth became clear to him in an instant. Not only had her husband been a brute, he'd not known how to bring pleasure to his beautiful wife, or perhaps he couldn't be bothered. "Do you like that?" he asked.

Inhaling deeply, head flung back, she nodded.

Praying his resolve to go slowly wouldn't desert him, he lowered his head and suckled like a hungry babe. Slowly introducing this woman to the delights of sexual intimacy was suddenly of the utmost importance.

"This is more fun if we are both naked," he quipped, pushing the loosened gown off her hips. He took it as a good omen when she divested herself of the chemise. A costly pile of silk and taffeta swathed her feet. Only the corset and the pantalets stood in his way—although, perhaps not.

He scooped her up and carried her to the bed.

MAGGIE FLOATED in a sea of bliss, her fear gone. She lay on her back, watching Edouard take off his trousers and his unmentionables. The thick lance that sprang forth confirmed her suspicion he'd been gifted with physical endowments that made Fred's boasting laughably pathetic. It was hard to believe she was staring at a mere mortal. "You'll have to help me undo the corset," she said nervously, surprised words actually emerged from her dry throat.

"Keep it on," he replied, shaking his head as he lifted one knee onto the bed. "It's arousing."

It was also flattering, and she felt more comfortable with its flimsy protection. It pushed up her breasts in a provocative manner she rather liked.

She felt his warmth when he joined her on the bed, gradually relaxing as pangs of desire spiraled up her thighs and into her womb when he touched her nipples with his fingers. His lips and tongue then worked their magic.

She sifted her fingers through his silky hair as he suckled first one breast, then the other.

She relished every second. This is what had been missing with her husband. Euphoria. For the first time in her life, she was a desirable woman.

She faltered when he narrowed his eyes. "Your husband marked you," he growled.

She'd forgotten the faint bruises. "Yes."

"Coward," he hissed, stretching out beside her, looking up at the ceiling. "I give you my word I will never raise my hand against you."

"I believe you," she replied truthfully, rising up on one elbow so she had a better view of the size and thickness of the male member jutting out from its nest of black curls. It was as if he and Fred belonged to two different species.

"Do you want to touch me?" he rasped.

"More than anything, but..."

He took her hand and placed it on his manhood. "No buts, *ma chère*. Your caress will bring me pleasure."

"I don't know..."

"Trust your instinct," he said, folding his hands behind his head.

~

EDOUARD KNEW WHAT HE LIKED. Time was money to the mistresses he'd known in Paris and London, so he'd taught them how to please him quickly. It was about release, nothing more.

With Maggie, he intended to take his time. He wanted her to discover where and how he liked to be touched and looked forward to learning her body's secrets.

Probably unaware the crotchless pantalets revealed a tantalizing glimpse of her most private place, Maggie sat cross-legged beside him and moved her hand on his cock. She watched him, tightening her grip and pumping faster at just the right moment. He found most women superficial, but suspected Maggie was an intriguing puzzle he could spend years unraveling. He growled when she cupped his sac with her free hand. The hint of uncertainty in her eyes made him feel he was being touched by a virgin.

The notion heightened his arousal. She'd come close to release when he'd suckled her and he was ready to explode. He turned his head to look at her, awed by the glistening pink folds of her woman's place. He brushed his knuckles over the curls at her mons. "Perfect," he rasped as his balls drew up.

She moaned when his thumb found the swollen diamond of her desire. Her hand matched the rhythm of his strokes, faster and faster until she screamed her release at the moment his seed erupted. Basking in euphoria, he slipped a finger inside her as she convulsed, teasing the inner muscles to prolong her ecstasy. When she calmed, he gathered her into his embrace and savored the little aftershocks and contented sighs. He was humbled to have brought her to what he suspected was her first sexual climax.

Maggie drifted in uncharted waters. Even in the early years of her marriage, she'd never experienced the breathtaking cataclysm Edouard's touch had wrought. Safe in his strong arms, she relished the heat of his skin, the rise and fall of his chest, the aroma of male essence. The scent of male sperm normally turned her stomach. Now, she wanted to taste him. Witnessing the eruption from his magnificent body had tipped her over the edge into an ecstatic free-fall.

Did he realize he'd ignited an inferno—in her heart and her loins? Still in a fog of sexual satisfaction, she wasn't confident coherent words would emerge from her mouth, but she had to try. "I ...er ...that was ..."

He tilted her chin to his gaze. "I understand, *cherie*. For me too. It will be even better when we join our bodies."

She was tempted to beg him to take her now, without delay, but he was right. It was too soon and a murderer still threatened their happiness.

Chapter 16

Motive

Marcus and his constable spent a tedious afternoon questioning the members of the small orchestra. Frequent interruptions by scenery shifters rendered the curtained stage unsuitable for interviews, so they waylaid each player as he entered the hall on his way to the pit. Marcus had requested they arrive earlier than usual. He recognized the first to arrive as the conductor but Walsh approached him. "You're the band leader?" he asked.

The bald musician bristled. "We're an orchestra, not a band," he replied, his bulbous nose in the air.

Marcus sighed. This wasn't a good way to begin. "Our apologies," he said, gesturing to a chair. "This won't take long."

Clearly unaware he'd offended the chap, Walsh pulled out his notebook. "Please state your full name and occupation."

"Morris Johann Sebastian Ince. Conductor."

Marcus resisted the urge to snort, but Walsh dutifully scribbled down the information, evidently not appreciating the irony in the pretentious name.

"Your parents were musicians?" Marcus asked, quickly wishing he hadn't when Ince reeled off a list of his late father's musical accomplishments, the most notable of which seemed to be that he played the French horn in the Salford Brass Band. "Impressive, and you are carrying on his legacy by conducting the orchestra for the performers here."

"Exactly, though Chadwick never appreciated my talents."

"What makes you say that?"

"I often suggested changes to the music that would enhance the experience for the audience. I composed new songs for Mrs. Chadwick, for example."

"And Mr. Chadwick rejected your ideas."

"The man had no ear for music," Ince replied with a sigh. "And no willingness to listen to others' opinions about how to improve the music hall. Mrs. Chadwick is more amenable to my efforts. She used one of my songs for the reopening. The audience loved it."

"Did you resent your boss?"

"I hated him," Ince admitted. "More and more as time went on."

"Did you kill him?" Walsh asked, earning a glare from Marcus.

The musician straightened his shoulders and lifted his chin. "No. I was afraid of him, and he knew it. I stayed out of his way as much as possible."

Marcus believed him. "Thank you. You may go. Please send your members one at a time."

"You should arrest that Frenchman," Ince said as he rose. "Bad blood there. We all saw it."

Seemingly spared pretentious names, the rest of the orchestra—from the drummer to the oboist to the violinist—all expressed dislike and fear of Fred Chadwick. To a man, they suspected Deschanel, though none had any proof to offer other than the fight.

Exasperated by the lack of progress, Marcus asked Walsh's opinion.

"No harmony between any of them and Chadwick," his constable quipped with a smile.

Marcus groaned inwardly. It was definitely time to call it a day. "Who's left?" he asked.

Walsh consulted his list. "The juggler, the magician, the impersonator, the comic pianists, the comedian, the monologist, the tap dancer, the mime ..."

"Good grief!" Marcus exclaimed. "We're getting nowhere fast."

Maggie and Edouard were strolling arm in arm along Deansgate. They'd just reached Churchgate when they saw the Inspector and his constable exit *The Hippodrome*. "I'm tempted to pretend we haven't seen them," she said, worried the perceptive Inspector would guess they'd spent an intimate afternoon together.

"Might look suspicious," he replied. "They've seen us."

"Mrs. Chadwick," the Inspector said when they reached the theater. "Mr. Deschanel."

"Inspector Halliwell," they replied. "Constable Walsh."

There was an awkward moment of silence until Maggie remembered something she'd been curious about. "Have you managed to get into my husband's office?" she asked.

The red-faced policemen looked at each other, seemingly taken off guard by the question. "His office?"

"Yes, at the end of the corridor. Fred always kept it locked."

"Do you have a key?"

"I'm afraid not. I was forbidden to enter."

The Inspector's eyes widened. "You've never been inside?"

"No."

"Well, Walsh, I think it's time we investigated this office. Do you have a few minutes, Mrs. Chadwick?"

Maggie's face heated. She had hoped to spend more time with Edouard. "Yes, lots of time," she replied, resisting the urge to wink at Edouard who was no doubt grinning from ear to ear.

"Somebody must have a key," Halliwell said when they reached the office door.

"Fred didn't trust anybody," Maggie replied.

"Wait," Walsh exclaimed. "There was a key in his pocket when we found the body."

"And where is it now?" the Inspector asked, clearly exasperated.

"At HQ, Sir. I thought it important to log as evidence."

"We may as well try to get in since we're here," Edouard suggested, earning a nod from Halliwell.

"Put your shoulder to it, Walsh," the Inspector instructed.

"I'll help," Edouard said.

The two men almost fell into the room when the lock splintered. Maggie could scarcely believe the opulence of her husband's office. It stood in sharp contrast to the poverty of her flat. He'd probably had his way with other women on the plush chaise lounge. Tasteful landscape paintings adorned the walls. There was even a small private bar stocked with crystal glasses and what she recognized as expensive brands of gin, whisky and rum. But what captured her attention was the small safe, its door open and its contents gone.

"At least we now have a motive," Halliwell declared.

"But how did the killer open the safe?" Edouard asked.

Marcus scratched his head. "He either knew the combination, or he's a safe cracker."

"Or he forced Fred to open it," Maggie suggested.

"But the body was found in Mrs. Chadwick's dressing

room," Walsh said. "And how did the office door get locked again?"

"I don't know," Halliwell confessed.

"Mrs. Chadwick," Walsh said, flipping through his notebook. "Didn't you say earlier that Mr. Bandi usually met with your husband in his office?"

"Yes."

"So," the constable said, looking smugly pleased with himself. "He'd have known about the safe."

"And the key," Edouard added.

Chapter 17

The Mystery Deepens

Rajendra Bandi startled when the heavy door to his cell clanged open. He'd been trying unsuccessfully to nap on the hard bench that passed for a bed. Arms still folded to ward off the damp chill, he sat up, surprised to see Inspector Halliwell enter. "Wot can I do tha fer?" he asked, determined not to be cowed by the giant. So far, he'd not suffered violence at the hands of his jailers, but a man of Indian extraction had to expect he'd be beaten sooner or later.

He didn't sense violence in Halliwell, but the young constable who entered after him was a different matter. Rajendra recognized the type after years of dealing with the police. He'd not think twice about using his fists.

"Have you ever been inside Fred Chadwick's office, Mr. Bandi?" the Inspector asked.

Rajendra had to tread very carefully, lest he implicate himself. "On occasion. Like I said, I paid rent. Bloody exorbitant. 'E preferred to do business away fra' pryin' eyes in the 'all."

"I assume you paid him cash, so what did he do with the money after you gave it to him?"

"Bugger if I knows. 'E shoved me out reet away and locked the door."

"Did he unlock the door to let you in when you went to his office?"

"Aye. Kept the key in 'is pocket."

Rajendra thought things were going smoothly until the constable loomed over him and fisted his hands in the front of his prison overalls.

"Listen, creep, we've got you dead to rights for operating an opium den and running illegal cock and dog fights. Why not just confess to murdering Chadwick and stealing the contents of the safe?"

"Nay," Rajendra replied, struggling to be free of the constable's grip. "I admit to my crimes, but killin' Fred Chadwick ain't one ov 'em."

Halliwell put a restraining hand on his constable's shoulder. "You're saying you never watched him open the safe?"

"Too reet. Chadwick were a cagey bugger. Didn't trust nobody."

"But you knew he had a safe in the office," Walsh insisted, stepping away.

"Aye, but 'e were bigger 'an me. 'E'd a kilt me if ..."

Halliwell waved him to silence. "Do you have any thoughts as to the identity of the killer?"

Rajendra should perhaps admit he knew the murderer's identity, but there was no profit in doing so. "My money's on the missus," he lied.

"You think Mrs. Chadwick had the strength to garrote her husband?"

Rajendra shook his head. "She must 'ave had 'elp."

Confident he'd deflected suspicion away from himself, Rajendra settled back onto the bench as he watched the policemen leave his cell. Having caught a glimpse of the killer's back when he went to pay Fred his share of the takings, he knew Maggie Chadwick wasn't guilty. Let the police chase their tails for a while. They evidently thought the murderer had stolen the money. Only Rajendra knew the murderer hadn't been interested in the cash. He must have done the deed after Fred opened the safe, then dragged his body to the dressing room. Perhaps he'd not had time to go back and empty the safe. Or maybe he simply wanted to kill Fred, which was completely understandable.

Rajendra had to hope the police didn't find out about his warehouse near the River Croal. If Halliwell found the cash stashed there, he'd for sure think Rajendra guilty of murder. He should have left well enough alone, but the temptation had been too great—an open safe, a ton of money just sitting there for the taking.

Being banged up in this godforsaken cell made it difficult to let the real murderer know he knew his identity and the reason for his crime. A little blackmail money wouldn't go amiss.

～

"Guilty as sin, I'd say," Walsh opined when they left the cells.

"He's hiding something, I'll grant you that," Marcus agreed, glad to be out of the fetid place. "However, I doubt he's the killer. He probably had a lucrative business going in the cellar. Why would he risk exposing his operation to the scrutiny of the law?"

Walsh scratched his bushy sideburns, seemingly deep in thought, but made no reply.

Marcus thought back over the interview. "Bandi was only too willing to lay the blame on Maggie Chadwick but didn't provide any proof or reason for his opinion."

"I wouldn't normally trust anything the wog says, but it's looking more and more likely the wife was involved," Walsh countered. "We haven't been able to locate anyone else with a motive. Her husband beat her and never shared the profits with her, so ..."

"Yes, but how did she get him to open the safe?"

"She has obviously taken a lover. Maybe the Frenchman threatened him."

"With what? A length of wire? If the murderer had a weapon why not use it instead of a garrote? We already know from witness accounts that Chadwick and Deschanel were evenly matched when it came to a physical confrontation. It doesn't make sense."

Walsh scratched his head. "Or, the wife and her lover burst into the office and surprised him with the safe open," he suggested.

"But he always locked the door. It took two of you to bust it open today. Chadwick would have closed the safe immediately if he heard someone trying to break in, wouldn't he?"

Walsh shook his head. "It's a mystery, sir."

"That's the reason we need to be good at our job, my lad."

Chapter 18

Balls In The Air

Marcus decided his enquiries might yield better results if he conducted interviews away from the theater. The barrack-like atmosphere of the offices of the Bolton Borough Police was intimidating. After a long tirade about Marcus's failure to make an arrest, the Superintendent grudgingly allowed him to use a small room where he and Walsh could question the rest of the performers.

"Who's first?" he asked Walsh, squeezing into his seat behind a scarred table brought in from the canteen.

"Douglas Sudren, the juggler."

"Fetch him."

Walsh ushered in a surprisingly elderly man who looked frail enough to be blown over by a gust of wind.

"You're the juggler at *The Hippodrome?*" Marcus asked, hoping he didn't sound too doubtful.

Sudren eyed the chair provided for him, but didn't sit. "Aye, for many a year."

"Sit down, please," Marcus said.

Sudren looked round the cramped space nervously. "I prefer to stand."

Then he sat.

Marcus had always been under the impression jugglers were men with great powers of concentration who could keep a dozen balls in the air at one time. Sudren seemed distracted and nervous.

"Can you tell us anything about the murder of Fred Chadwick?"

"Orlando Grossmith's your man," Sudren replied with great conviction.

Marcus glanced at Walsh who looked as puzzled as he felt.

"Orlando Grossmith?"

"The comic pianist. Never did trust the man. What kind of a name is Orlando? Only a criminal would have such a name."

"I see," Marcus replied, tempted to send the old fool packing. "And do you have any evidence to support this accusation?"

"Grossmith hated Chadwick."

Walsh snorted. "We've yet to interview anyone who didn't hate him."

"True. He bullied all of us."

"So, did you hate him?"

"Of course. We all did."

Marcus gritted his teeth. "Thank you, Mr. Sudren. That will be all."

The tap dancer came next. Felipe Gonzalez turned out to be a very handsome young Spaniard who spoke almost no English. The few words he did speak were a curious mixture of Lancashire dialect and foreign accent. In broken English, he claimed he'd spent the entire night of the murder in bed with Sally Fry, the part-time waitress. Asked if she would corroborate his alibi, he winked and exclaimed, "She will remember."

"Cocky bastard," Walsh sneered after the Spaniard left. "The monologist is next, sir."

Marcus sighed. Eliminating suspects was progress, he supposed. But they were no closer to tracking down the killer.

Surprisingly, Ernest Holloway turned out to be the most interesting performer. Marcus expected a former schoolteacher or retired academic. Holloway was a spinner who'd grown weary of working in a cotton mill. "Awful place, a mill," he told Marcus. "Luckily, I were taught to read and write, so I left the mill and tried me 'and at summat more fun."

"But surely you could make more money in the mill," Marcus replied.

"Money ain't everythin'," Holloway countered. "I'm 'appier doin' me bit in the music 'all."

"Even working for Fred Chadwick?"

"Chadwick were a bully, reet enough, but I allus remind my kiddies about the tale o' the three little pixies and the wolf. The wolf gets 'is due in the end."

Marcus was surprised Holloway could support a family on a performer's wages. "You have children?" he asked.

Holloway grinned. "Me and the missus 'ave seven kiddies and another on the way."

"Blimey!" Walsh exclaimed after the monologist was sent on his way. "Seven kids!"

Marcus had mixed feelings about the interview. "He's possibly the happiest man I ever met," he said, all the while lamenting the family he might have had with Eliza.

"I doubt he'd risk what he has by killing Chadwick," Walsh mused.

"You're right. He has no motive. We can eliminate him from our list."

"You seem preoccupied," Maggie told Edouard.

He felt badly. They were again enjoying lunch in his apartment and he'd wanted it to be as special as the previous day. However, she was right. "I'm pondering how best to track down your husband's killer," he admitted.

She put down her fork. "I wish you would leave that to the police."

"I can't. You and I will be the prime suspects until the murderer is found."

"But, if the guilty party is some random outsider who broke in, stole the cash and killed Fred, there's little hope of you solving the case."

He took hold of her trembling hand. "But don't you share my gut feeling the killer had intimate knowledge of the theater and Fred's routines?"

"I do," she confessed, meshing her elegant fingers with his. "You must tread carefully so as not to alert the killer."

Raising her hand to his lips, he nodded his agreement. "I dealt with dangerous men in Paris but someone proficient with a garrote is more than dangerous. There was something very personal in the manner of Fred's murder. It was vicious and vindictive. The killer had a score to settle. What had Fred done to give rise to such hatred?"

"My husband had many enemies, some he probably made on his frequent trips out of town. He treated everyone who worked at the theater badly and they loathed him as a result. However, with the exception of Ken Swales, they've all worked at *The Hippodrome* for years, so why kill Fred now?"

"I don't have an answer to that question. Tell me who at the theater has their finger on everything that goes on there?"

"Probably old Angus McCray, the stage manager. He goes about his business without any fuss and nobody pays much attention. But he's a canny Scot who doesn't miss much."

"He has a crew of helpers?"

"Yes. Different casual workers who come and go, but he only takes on men he thinks he can trust, and his instincts have never failed."

"Until now, perhaps."

~

MAGGIE SUGGESTED she introduce Edouard to Angus. "Otherwise, he's likely to tell you to mind your own business."

They entered the theater after a brisk walk from Deansgate and found Angus on his knees fiddling with the floodlights at the front of the stage. Breathing heavily, he got up slowly, wiped his hands on his overalls and shook Edouard's hand. "I check these fittings every day, ye ken. Canna be too careful wi' gas."

"We're all grateful you pay attention to these details," Maggie said, seeing no harm in stroking his ego.

"Fred thought it a waste o' time."

"My husband had no patience," she replied.

"Aye. So, ye've come to pick ma brain."

Edouard nodded. "Maggie assures me nothing goes on at *The Hippodrome* that you don't know about."

Angus winked at Maggie and chuckled. "Weel, 'tis exaggeratin' a wee bit, but I keep ma eyes open."

"So, what can you tell us?" Edouard asked.

"Bandi came late that night, probably to pay Fred his share of ill-gotten gains from the cellar. He kept to the shadows so the charladies wouldna see him."

"How do you know this?"

Angus pointed to the rigging high above the stage. "'Tis amazing what ye can see from up yonder."

Looking up, Edouard nodded. "Especially when nobody knows you're up there."

"Do you think Bandi killed my husband?" Maggie asked.

"Weel, he rushed out o' here like a bat out o' hell, stuffin' bank notes in his pockets."

Maggie gasped. "He murdered Fred, then stole the contents of the safe."

Angus shook his head. "He stole the money, but that weasel wouldna hae the guts to kill a mon. Besides, Fred saw somebody in the corridor leadin' to his office before Bandi came. He shouted *Oy* when he saw whoever 'twas."

"So," Edouard said. "That person got him to open the safe, then killed him, but didn't take the cash."

"I reckon so," Angus agreed. "Strange, aye?"

"Did you see this person?" Maggie asked.

"Wish I had, dear lady, but nay. I didna hae the courage to leave the safety o' the riggin'. I'm sorry."

Maggie kissed the old man's forehead. "Don't be sorry. We appreciate your help."

"Aye, ye'd best find the culprit, else ye and this Frenchie will likely remain the prime suspects."

Chapter 19

Magic And Music

After sipping a fortifying cup of tea, Marcus was about to resume his interrogation of the performers when he received a note, ostensibly from Maggie Chadwick. "The stage manager claims Bandi stole the money from the safe, but isn't the killer," he told Walsh.

"Sounds unlikely," his constable replied. "What does he base his theory on?"

"He apparently observed Bandi fleeing with the money from up in the rigging above the stage."

"Interesting, so it's likely he's the murderer."

"But this McCray fellow corroborates the charlady's assertion that Chadwick shouted *Oy* at somebody before Bandi arrived."

For the first time since the investigation began, Marcus felt a touch of optimism. New details were coming to light. "We'll have another chat with Mr. Bandi. He's not going anywhere. In the meantime, who's next?"

"The pianists, Orlando Grossmith and George Parry."

"Let's hope we get some reasonable information from them."

His hopes faltered when the two men preceded Walsh into the interview room. He'd heard the term *macaroni* applied to foppishly dressed, aristocratic young men. Still, it was his job to establish the facts, not judge people's fashion sense.

"Please be seated, gentlemen," he said politely.

"Orlando Grossmith," one replied, offering his hand.

"George Parry," said the other as he too offered his hand.

Faced with two outthrust hands, Marcus couldn't help but notice the well-manicured fingernails of both men. It was unlikely either of them could garrote a man; they might break a nail. He repeated his request that they be seated.

Pouting, they complied.

"We're Grossmith ..."

"And Parry."

"Comic ..."

"Pianists."

The pair wiggled their fingers as if playing imaginary pianos.

Standing behind the silly duo, Walsh grinned, which didn't help Marcus stifle the laughter bubbling in his throat. "Can you shed any light on the murder?" he asked.

"Good ..."

"... riddance."

"Everybody ..."

"... hated the bully."

Marcus filled his lungs, praying for patience. "Do you suspect anyone in particular?"

"Well," Grossmith began.

Despite his best efforts, Marcus' attention shifted to Parry for the next salvo.

"We love her, but ..."

"... Maggie had every reason ..."

"... to kill the brute."

"You think she garroted her husband?" Walsh asked.

"The Frenchman ..."

"... garroted him."

Beginning to understand why someone might be driven to throttle another person, Marcus asked, "Do you have evidence to support this accusation?"

"It's ..."

"... obvious."

"Isn't it?"

Marcus was grateful when Walsh took it upon himself to usher the foppish pair out of the room.

HAVING DISCOVERED from Maggie that the theater's magician, Alexander the Great, occupied a flat on Deansgate, not far from his store, Edouard called on him on his way home. The middle-aged man purported to be French and spoke accented English throughout his performance. When he opened the door to his flat, Edouard extended his hand and addressed him accordingly. *"Je m'appelle Edouard Deschanel. Puis-je vous poser quelques questions sur votre travail au théâtre?"*

The magician's puzzled expression made it immediately obvious he didn't speak French. "Don't speak the lingo, I'm afraid," he replied. "All part of the act."

"I'm Edouard Deschanel, proprietor of *Shangri-La. May I come in and ask you a few questions?"*

"I know who you are. Any friend of Maggie's is a friend of mine. I'm Alex Proctor. Come in."

Two things took Edouard by surprise when he entered the flat. He prided himself on keeping his own apartment in good order, but the magician's home was immaculate. The place almost looked like nobody lived there. He was also surprised to see the man's young assistant, though she wasn't dressed in her usual flimsy costume. Nor did she show any lingering aftereffects of having been locked in a box and run through with swords. He was taken aback when the magician introduced her as his wife. Given the obvious age difference, he'd assumed she was perhaps Alexander's daughter. "Please, call me Angela," she insisted, shaking his hand firmly. "Won't you sit down?"

"You want to ask me about Fred Chadwick's murder," Alex said.

"Yes. As you can imagine, Maggie and I are anxious to find out who killed her husband."

"Because it's likely the peelers think you did it."

"Exactly. Do you have any information that could be useful?"

"We didn't have much to do with Fred," Alex said. "He tried it on with my wife just once and I told him I would wave my magic wand and make him disappear just like that." He snapped his fingers for effect.

"Did he pay heed to your warning?"

"Never bothered either of us again," Angela said.

"He seems to have been universally hated."

"I didn't particularly like him," Alex said. "But I didn't hate him."

"It's puzzling. The whole ensemble disliked him, but they've all tolerated his bullying for years. Why kill him now?"

"That's not quite correct," Alex replied. "Ken Swales was only recently hired as the comedian. He's a poor replacement for Billy Guest, God rest him. Can't see Swales lasting long. His jokes aren't funny. I suppose Fred was in a bind and hired the first joker that came along."

"This Billy Guest died?" Edouard asked.

"Very suddenly. Heart gave out, the doctor said," Angela explained. "He was truly a funny man."

Satisfied he'd at least gleaned a snippet of new information, Edouard thanked his hosts and prepared to leave. "One last word of advice," he said. "I wouldn't mention to Inspector Halliwell that you once threatened to make Chadwick disappear."

"Too late," Alex replied with a chuckle. "Already told him earlier today when I was called to the police station for an interview. I also had to admit I learned how to pick locks when I worked as an escape artist years ago."

~

EDOUARD CAME DIRECTLY to Maggie's dressing room after meeting with Alex and Angela. She listened intently to the account of his meeting with the magician. "I'd forgotten about the comedian," she admitted. "I suppose we were all so shocked by Billy's sudden death, then Swales turned up out of the blue and Fred hired him to fill the void."

"Without an audition?"

"I don't know. Fred didn't care much about the quality of the performances, so long as people kept paying to come to the theater."

"From the moans and groans, I'd say most of the audience doesn't think Swales is funny."

"He isn't. Fred would eventually have sacked him when somebody better came along."

"If Swales knew he was going to be sent packing, it would give him a motive."

"Not a good one, though."

"True," he admitted, putting his arms around her waist. "I think Fred knew it was you who drew the crowds. The people love you. It's Miss Maggie they come to see."

She shook her head. "They enjoy singing along with me, but it's the variety of acts they like."

"I wouldn't have come a second time if you hadn't waltzed onto the stage and captured my heart," he confessed, looking into her brown eyes.

Maggie wished she felt confident that his infatuation would last. She had so little experience of men. She'd placed her trust in Fred and look where that had led. "We should take things slowly," she said. "At least until this nightmare is over."

"I understand your reluctance to trust me," he said. "But I am not like Fred. I won't hurt you."

She knew he wasn't a violent man, but she was close to losing her heart to him. Would he hold it safe?

Chapter 20

An Arrest

Marcus groaned inwardly when the Superintendent entered the cramped room while he was questioning the mime whose name was Trevor Coleman. They only knew that much because the reed-thin man had written it down in Walsh's notebook when required to give his name. From that point on, Coleman insisted on staying in character. When asked if he suspected anyone of killing Chadwick, he stuck out his tongue, swiped a finger across his throat, rolled his eyes, shrugged and shook his head. Indeed, the shrug and the head-shake were offered in response to every subsequent question.

The interview was a farce. Arms folded across his chest, the scowling Superintendent became more and more agitated as it progressed, so Marcus wasn't surprised to be summoned to his superior's office immediately after Coleman was sent on his way.

He told himself to stay calm while the Superintendent berated the lack of progress. It seemed useless to point out they were, in fact, making progress. Several people had been eliminated from suspicion.

"Walsh tells me Bandi is your prime suspect."

Marcus clenched his jaw. His constable had a thing or two to learn about loyalty. "Mr. Bandi probably stole Chadwick's money, but ..."

"Then he's the killer."

"The stage manager said ..."

"Bandi's Indian. You can't trust those people."

Marcus' throat tightened, but he kept silent. He doubted his opinion would carry any weight in the face of his superior officer's prejudices.

"Arrest him."

A sick feeling swept over Marcus. "He's already in custody on a charge of ..."

"Charge him with murder. The general public will be relieved we've made an arrest."

Marcus was dismissed with a wave of the hand. His belly in knots, he left the office. The public wouldn't be too pleased when they discovered the wrong man had been charged. It was to be hoped the real culprit was found before Bandi paid the ultimate price.

MAGGIE WAS of the opinion the theater's impressionist might know more about Ken Swales. "The comedian shares a dressing room with Harry, so they may have got to know each other," she told Edouard.

As luck would have it, Edouard found Harry Little alone in the dressing room. He introduced himself, though Harry said there was no need. "I know who you are," he said. "I expect you're nervous about coming under suspicion."

Edouard decided to shrug off the comment. "I suppose we're all suspects until they find the killer."

"But you have motive, dear boy," Harry replied, sounding remarkably like Benjamin Disraeli.

"That's spot on," Edouard told him.

"And you've climbed *the greasy pole* in the world of *Bon Marché*," Harry quipped, using the politician's favorite saying.

Edouard smiled. "What can you tell me about Ken Swales?"

Harry looked down his nose and thrust out his chest. "We are not amused," he said, imitating Her Majesty to a tee.

"Seriously. What do you make of him?"

Harry tucked a hand into his waistcoat, retrieved a tricorne from a rack of costumes and declared, "A cold fish. Send him to meet his Waterloo."

"I'm enjoying your impressions," Edouard said, feeling the interview was going nowhere. "But do you know anything about Swales?"

"No, but Joe Peel might."

"Goliath?"

"They're both from Blackrod."

"Look," Rajendra said, his knees trembling and his gut in knots when the Inspector came to charge him with murder. "I'll admit to thievin' the money and I'll tell thee where to find it, but somebody else killed Chadwick. I'm not a murderer."

The constable gritted his teeth and clenched his fists. "You expect us to believe that?"

Rajendra braced himself for the first blow, but breathed again when the Inspector intervened. "You claim the safe was open?"

"Aye."

"And the office wasn't locked?"

"No, which were strange. Chadwick never left it unlocked."

"So, how did it come to be locked when we tried to enter?" Walsh asked.

"It's a Chubb deadlock. It activated when I closed the door as I left."

Walsh sneered. "You paid close attention."

"In my line of work, you notice such things," Rajendra admitted.

"Where's the money now?" Halliwell asked.

"Stashed in a warehouse I rent near the Croal. Knowsley Street. Number 47."

"Cuff him," the Inspector told his constable. "He can show us."

As he left the prison cell with the policemen, Rajendra sensed the Inspector believed he was innocent of murder. If not, he could always rely on fellow Hindus from the temple to confirm his alibi. He only hoped it would be enough to save him from the noose. The irony struck him full force. After a lifetime of involvement in criminal enterprises, he might be hanged for a crime he hadn't committed.

Marcus trudged wearily up five flights of stone steps of a dilapidated warehouse built at least a century ago beside the River Croal. This was an aspect of police work he hated. A stern-faced Walsh waited at the top, his hand clamped on Bandi's shoulder. The constable wasn't even out of breath, whereas Marcus was feeling his age. "This had better not be a wild goose chase," he warned Bandi.

"Nah. Tha'll see."

Their prisoner had told them the door was secured with padlock and chain, but he'd surrendered the key at the time of his arrest. The key was nowhere to be found in the police station, but Walsh made short work of the chain with the bolt cutters he'd brought then pushed Bandi into an enormous empty space—empty that is except for a small safe in one corner. Marcus assumed this was where Bandi normally stored the boxes of patriotic paraphernalia. Very little daylight penetrated the filth on the barred windows set high in the wall, but that didn't seem to hinder Bandi as he knelt to turn the combination dial.

When the door of the safe opened, Walsh shoved Bandi out of the way and reached inside. Marcus could tell without counting it that his constable held a small fortune and suspected not all of it was from the theft at *The Hippodrome*.

Marcus held open the bag he'd brought and Walsh stuffed the money into it.

"Tha's teckin' it all?" Bandi asked.

"Yes," Marcus replied. "Do you have any objection?"

"S'pose not," the sulking Indian replied.

Maggie's emotions see-sawed as she tried to make sense of the news Edouard brought. "But Angus said Bandi couldn't be guilty," she cried. "I never trusted the horrible little man, but if he's innocent ..."

"It's the worst possible scenario," Edouard agreed. "If they hang an innocent man, the real killer is still free."

"Do you think Halliwell truly believes he's apprehended the murderer?"

"Hard to say. You explained in the note you sent to him that Fred apparently saw someone else near the office before Bandi even arrived."

"We must speak to the Inspector."

"Yes. We need to tell him about the Blackrod connection between Goliath and Swales."

Maggie felt more confused than ever. "I suppose. Although why that should be important, I can't imagine."

Chapter 21

New Line-Up

Before Fred's death, Maggie's life followed a predictable path. She performed, she mingled with the patrons, then she went home. If Fred shared her bed at night, she was too nervous to sleep. If he didn't come home, resentment kept her churning all night.

Only gin softened the bitter edges of exhaustion and unhappiness.

Her new life was equally exhausting, but in a good way. She still performed every night, except Sunday, and invested a lot of time with the other performers discussing how to improve their acts. She took over management of the hall, holding frequent meetings with Angus and Emerson about the best way to proceed. She discovered she had a good head for business, and it was gratifying to see profits mount.

But the best part of her new life was spending the afternoon naked in bed with Edouard after lunch at his apartment.

Drunk on her new lover, she didn't need the gin bottle.

Sexual congress with Fred had always been a brief, unsatisfactory, and sometimes terrifying affair. With Edouard, making love meant just that. He knew exactly how and where to make her body respond to his touch. Thanks to his whispered, risqué compliments, she began to believe she was an attractive woman. She loved having her breasts and other intimate places suckled.

He taught her what he enjoyed and she craved taking his magnificent manhood into her mouth. She learned the French word for *cock*, and longed for the day he could thrust his hard *bite* inside her and they would finally be one.

EDOUARD SHOULD BE SPENDING MORE time taking care of *Shangri-La* business, but afternoons spent making love with Maggie were a drug he couldn't give up. He'd enjoyed sexual congress with women in Paris and London, but he'd never before experienced the euphoria Maggie brought to their lovemaking.

He fell into the habit of accompanying her to the theater after their trysts and always stayed to watch her performance. He couldn't get enough of her and longed for the day he could thrust inside her. His treacherous first wife had soured him on marriage, but he found himself contemplating a permanent future with Maggie.

But first, a killer had to be brought to justice. Bandi had been falsely accused, which meant it was incumbent upon Edouard to track down the real culprit.

At Angus McCray's suggestion, Maggie had decided to change the order of the performances. All the artists agreed that, as the star of the show, she should perform last. The new line up proved popular and word spread quickly. For the first time in anyone's memory, *The Hippodrome* had to turn people away at the door.

Before the changes, he returned to Maggie's dressing room after watching her perform and they strolled to her flat together.

Now, intrigued by what he had learned about the comedian, he was glad of the opportunity to stay to watch the whole show. "I hope his jokes have improved," he told Maggie before leaving her dressing room to find his favorite table.

"Don't count on it," she replied.

It was the first time Edouard had sat through the new program. Along with everyone else in attendance, he applauded the creative twist at the end of Goliath's act. In a charming bit of pantomime, a diminutive David, played by none other than Maria dressed as a boy, laid the giant low—not with a sling but with Cupid's arrow.

Harry Little added new impressions to his repertoire which the audience immediately recognized. They laughed and shouted encouragement when the mime pretended to be trapped inside a box. People held their breath when the frail juggler tossed flaming torches in the air, and the crowd went wild when Alexander the Great's lovely assistant emerged unscathed after he sawed her in half. Everyone sang along when the comic pianists added a couple of popular new tunes. The chorus line ended their performance with a tantalizing view of wiggling bottoms as they took a bow with their backs to the audience and skirts raised.

Next came a new act, a *lion comique* by the name of Ken Rayburn. A hush fell when the dandy swaggered onstage. The Proctors had recommended Rayburn. Edouard had seen similar performers strut their stuff in London. Maggie was banking on the act becoming popular in Bolton. Edouard wasn't sure if *The Hippodrome's* patrons would appreciate Rayburn's glossy top hat, dandified clothing and champagne glass. Like everyone else in the theater, he held his breath as the pianist played the opening bars of the song.

∾

Oh, gather 'round, my jolly friends, and lend a
  cheery ear,
I'll sing a tale of dapper days, where lions roam
  quite near.
In London town, where gaslights gleam, and
  cobblestones abound,
The lion comique takes the stage, with a mighty,
  playful sound.

~

MOUTHS FELL OPEN. The rich, baritone voice had taken everyone by surprise.

~

Roar, roar, hear the dandy call,
In the music hall, he stands so tall.
With a swagger in his step and a wink of his eye,
The roaring dandy, oh my, oh my!

~

OH MY, the laughing audience shouted.

~

In top hat fine and waistcoat bright, he struts
  upon the stage,
A winking eye and charming grin, the lion steals
  the rage.
He sings of love and merry nights, of follies and
  delights,

With every note, the crowd erupts, beneath the gaslit lights.

~

ROAR, *roar...*

~

THE AUDIENCE ROARED WITH RAYBURN, and had no trouble joining in the chorus. They applauded loudly when he doffed his top hat, took his bow and raised his champagne glass.

Relieved, Edouard was enjoying himself immensely when Ken Swales came onstage. The booing began almost immediately, and the reason soon became apparent.

"Why do cows wear bells?" Swales asked.

"Because their horns don't work," the audience groaned.

Undeterred, Swales soldiered on, apparently having no sense of timing, nor of the mood of his audience. "Why are pirates called pirates?"

"They just ARRR," came the reply.

And so it went—one stale joke after the other until the comedian was booed off the stage.

The punters knew Miss Maggie came next and they weren't willing to tolerate Swales any longer.

Edouard stood and applauded with everyone else when Maggie appeared. His body reacted predictably to her charming smile and infectious talent. But he couldn't shake the feeling there was something odd about Swales.

Maggie was well into her second song when it struck him. The man claimed to be a comedian but he never smiled once. In fact, he seemed bored with the entire proceedings.

Being last on the bill meant Maggie's performance ended much later than before, so she was glad of Edouard's company as she walked home through the poorly lit streets.

"You impress me more every time I watch you," he said as they turned the corner into Bank Street.

"You'll tire of me someday," she replied, still unsure of his willingness to commit to her.

He stopped abruptly and took her into his arms. "*Non, chérie.* Stop selling yourself short," he growled. "I will never tire of you."

She melted into his strength. "I'm sorry. It's simply that ..."

"I am *not* Fred Chadwick," he replied. "Surely you know by now you can trust me."

The sincerity in his dark eyes convinced her. "I suppose I'm just in knots over the police investigation."

"Tomorrow, we'll take Angus to the police station with us and make it clear to Halliwell he's got the wrong man."

"And we'll ask Goliath if he knows anything about Swales."

"Good plan," he agreed after bestowing an arousing kiss on her lips.

Arm in arm, they continued their walk to her flat. He escorted her up the stairs and made sure she was safely inside before he left to walk home.

Chapter 22

Falsely Accused

When Angus McCray arrived at the police station and corroborated Bandi's claim someone else had been near Chadwick's office before him, Marcus had no choice but to have him repeat his testimony to the Superintendent. "Mr. McCray also bears out the charlady's assertion that she heard Mr. Chadwick yell at whoever it was," he explained.

The Superintendent thanked McCray effusively but his tone changed abruptly after the Scot left.

Resigned to bearing the brunt of the tirade about his incompetence now that the Indian had been cleared of the charge by an eyewitness, Marcus felt sorry for Walsh. He could almost smell his constable's anger and frustration as the Superintendent heaped blame on them both.

Had he not been dependent on the Superintendent for his livelihood, Marcus might have had the courage to point out that it was his superior officer who'd insisted Bandi be charged with murder.

It was of some consolation that he harbored a secret the Superintendent knew nothing about. True to his word, Bandi had led them to his hoard of cash. The safe hidden in the rented warehouse contained a small fortune.

When Mrs. Chadwick had arrived at the station earlier with Angus McCray, Marcus had taken great pleasure in handing over the bulk of the money to her. By rights, all the cash should have been logged as evidence, but such evidence tended to mysteriously disappear.

Convinced the money he gave her was more than even Fred had squirreled away, a shocked Maggie informed him she intended to distribute a goodly portion of it to the people employed in the music hall.

Marcus' delight at depriving his dimwitted superior officer of the chance to purloin the cash faltered when the Superintendent concluded his officious tirade with a brilliant conclusion. "Now, you'll have to arrest the obvious culprits—Mrs. Chadwick and her lover."

Sympathy for Walsh fled like a flock of startled birds. The constable was the only person who could have provided the Superintendent with private information about Maggie and Deschanel.

"It's an enormous relief," Maggie admitted to Edouard when they returned to his apartment from the police station.

"*Oui*," he replied. "It's hard to believe your husband hoarded so much money. It will be secure in the store's safe."

"And he never shared it with me," she said. "But I was actually talking about the murder charge being dropped against Bandi. I never liked him but an innocent man cannot hang for a crime he didn't commit."

"Of course. Now, we can follow up on the clues we've uncovered."

"I don't know how I feel about that," she confessed. "Perhaps we should leave the investigation to the police."

"But they're obviously getting nowhere. Walsh didn't even write down anything we told him about Swales."

"I noticed," she said, her thoughts in turmoil.

"The constable thinks you and I are guilty," he declared.

A chill crept up Maggie's spine. "I agree, though I don't believe the Inspector thinks we murdered Fred. I suppose Walsh's suspicions are a good enough reason to ask Goliath about Swales."

"Tomorrow," he replied. "Today, we should celebrate your windfall. Let's eat luncheon in *Shangri-La's* café."

She put her arms around his waist and pressed her mons against his arousal. "Celebrating sounds like a good idea, though I was thinking of something other than food."

He laughed. "*Méchante.* Be patient. We have all afternoon to celebrate after we eat."

He was right. Intimacy with Edouard had turned her into a *naughty girl* and she could never thank him enough.

Edouard loved flirting with Maggie; when he whispered the promise of sexual delights, her ready blush and laughing brown eyes never failed to arouse him. He understood why she found it difficult to trust a man, but was gratifyingly certain she was starting to trust him. As they enjoyed their luncheon in *Shangri-La's* café, the prospect of another afternoon spent frolicking naked with Maggie hardened his cock.

His euphoria died a quick death when he espied Halliwell and his sidekick speaking with the hostess. The Inspector's deep frown disturbed him. When the hostess pointed to Edouard, he knew.

"What's wrong?" Maggie asked as he rose abruptly and took her arm.

"I think we should meet the policemen at the door before they arrest me in front of my employees."

He'd have given anything to erase the fear from her eyes as she turned and saw the policemen. "But you're not the killer."

"Don't worry," he said, trying to sound unconcerned as they walked toward Halliwell. "We expected this might happen. I've been falsely accused before. It will soon be established that I'm innocent."

"Inspector," he said. "Will you allow me to see Mrs. Chadwick to my carriage, then I'll come quietly?"

He was grateful the policeman nodded despite his constable's angry demeanor.

~

Marcus harbored serious doubts about Deschanel's guilt, but he had no choice. After completing the unpleasant business of charging the Frenchman and seeing him locked away safely, he had a sinking feeling Mrs. Chadwick would be waiting in the station's drafty foyer to continue the harangue she'd begun at *Shangri-La*.

Marcus himself had lost his one true love to a fatal illness and recognized that tearing Deschanel and Maggie Chadwick apart would be just as heartbreaking. It was obvious they were in love. Fred Chadwick's death had been a blessing in disguise, but he doubted either of them had anything to do with the killing. Maggie deserved happiness after living with an abusive ne'er-do-well.

He vowed to continue investigating in the hope of bringing the murderer to justice, but he refrained from mentioning that in front of Walsh. His constable obviously thought Deschanel was guilty and apparently had the ear of the Superintendent. When Mrs. Chadwick rushed to speak with them, Walsh warned her, "You're just as guilty as he is, but Bandi claims he saw a man leaving the theater by the back door, so his testimony gets you off the hook—for the moment."

A mixture of indignation and fear crossed Maggie Chadwick's face, but she quickly recovered. "My husband decided to pick a fight with Mr. Deschanel simply because he visited my dressing room. The two had never met before and it was the first time I'd spoken to Edouard. Where's the motive?"

"We've only your word for all that," Walsh retorted. "It's obvious the two of you are lovers."

Maggie's deep blush betrayed her, but Marcus couldn't allow his subordinate to keep harassing her. "That's enough, Constable. I'll see Mrs. Chadwick to the door."

Chapter 23

Dilemma

Performing and keeping up the pretense that she was happy was the last thing Maggie wanted to do. She'd thought those days were over. Even returning to *The Hippodrome* filled her with foreboding. Indeed, a knot of dread had taken up permanent residence inside her. However, Edouard Deschanel was her future. If she didn't pull herself together and track down the real killer, there was no future. The police couldn't be counted on to continue the investigation if they thought they had the right man.

She had no friends to rely on—Fred had made sure of that.

Her fellow performers and the people who worked at the theater were her only family. She had to trust and confide in them, though one of them might be the murderer. Indications were that the killer was familiar with the theater and Fred's routines.

Feeling more confident once she'd donned her costume, she asked Angus to gather everyone together before the doors opened to the public.

"You should be aware," she began, desperate not to reveal

her fear. "Mr. Deschanel has been charged with my husband's murder."

Utter silence greeted the news. Did this mean they all believed he was guilty?

"Mr. Deschanel and I have recently become good friends," she said, deeming it wiser to ignore Emerson Dean's snort. "I am quite certain he is innocent, and I intend to prove it."

She let her gaze wander from one face to another, disappointed to glimpse no reaction. Nevertheless, she had to continue. "You have all been a tower of strength during this whole nightmare and I know you'll support me as we carry on entertaining people who need fun and laughter in their lives."

"Of course, we will," Angus shouted in reply. "We're a family."

Faint murmurs of agreement and a few nodding heads came as a bitter disappointment. Her hopes flagged.

The theater's mime startled everyone when he spoke into the silence. "Surely a man who owns a luxury store wouldn't risk it all by killing a nobody. We all know the Frenchman only recently started coming to *The Hippodrome*."

"Aye," came the chorus.

Maggie breathed again. Hope was alive. Their support made it easier to pass on to each of them a share of the money Halliwell had given her. She'd been reluctant to offer it before lest it be seen as a bribe.

"The police recovered the money stolen from Fred," she told them. "You all deserve a share of the proceeds you helped the theater to earn. I have five pounds for each of you."

Cheers greeted the news. She received many hearty hugs and effusive thanks as she doled out the cash retrieved from *Shangri-La's* safe. Only the comedian expressed no gratitude for the windfall.

MAGGIE'S GENEROSITY gave Emerson the opportunity to hug her for the very first time. She felt wonderful in his arms but he had to content himself with giving her a quick peck on the cheek.

He was grateful for the five pounds. Pomade was becoming more expensive. However, he'd worked at the theater longer than most, and serving a hall full of patrons was more taxing than selling cigarettes. Maria and Ken Swales were recent arrivals, yet they'd also received five pounds. It just didn't seem fair.

As for proving Deschanel's innocence, he didn't fancy her chances. In fact, he hoped the bugger was found guilty. Then the field would be open for him.

EDOUARD PACED THE TINY CELL. He'd expected the Inspector to come so they could discuss the situation rationally and he'd be released, but the hours had passed slowly with no sign of the presence of another human being, except for Bandi's occasional whining rant in a nearby cell.

The death of his wife in Paris had been resolved quickly. He was starting to fear this dilemma might drag on. Meanwhile, Maggie was on her own, no doubt worried to death. She'd want to do everything in her power to help him, and she was resilient, but what could a woman alone do? His innards knotted. There were risks involved in tracking down the real killer. He had to convince Halliwell to help her.

His fragile hopes were dashed when the cell door crashed open and Walsh entered, a billy club in his grip. The stern set of the constable's jaw was proof enough Edouard was in for a beating.

"Ready to confess?" Walsh demanded.

"I am not guilty so why would I confess?"

"You'll be singing a different tune by the time I'm done with you."

Edouard had been punched and kicked before, but he'd always been able to fight back. He braced himself for the inevitable when two burly policemen arrived and took hold of his arms.

WONDERING where Walsh had disappeared to, Marcus was on his way to Deschanel's cell when he heard the ruckus. The unmistakable sounds of violence spurred him to hurry. He didn't believe in beating confessions out of prisoners, unless their guilt was well established. He was all for avoiding an unnecessary trial when circumstances warranted it. This wasn't one of those circumstances.

When he reached the cell, his worst fear was confirmed. Teeth gritted, the Frenchman was held firm in the grip of two junior constables while Walsh laid into him.

He was disappointed in his assistant. The young man had potential, but he'd evidently gotten it into his head that Deschanel was guilty. Gut feelings were all very well, but a policeman had to make sure he had evidence to back up the charges. There was no such evidence to prove Deschanel had killed Chadwick.

However, the Superintendent wanted a conviction and Marcus would have his work cut out for him to find the real killer—or prove without a doubt that Deschanel was guilty. Whatever the case, he couldn't allow the beating of a prisoner who might be innocent. "Stop," he shouted, grasping Walsh's arm as he drew back to land another blow.

Truncheon raised, the constable whirled around, his face tight with anger.

For a moment, Marcus feared the young man might strike him, but he dropped his arm when he realized he was about to accost a superior officer. "What's going on here?" Marcus demanded of the two juniors who now stood to attention, having let their victim slump to the stone floor.

"Pick him up," he ordered. "Then go fetch the police physician."

They hefted Deschanel onto the bunk before making themselves scarce.

Marcus decided not to harangue Walsh in front of a prisoner. "You're dismissed," he hissed. "I'll speak to you later."

After the young man left, Deschanel sat up slowly. "My thanks, Inspector," he groaned, arms hugging his ribs.

"Anything broken?" Marcus asked, relieved Walsh had at least been careful to avoid hitting the prisoner's face.

"Only time will tell," the Frenchman replied. "However, it's Maggie who needs your help."

"How so?"

"She will try to expose the real killer. You must protect her."

Marcus had to admire Deschanel. He was clearly in a great deal of pain but his only thought was for the woman he loved. But he had to be sure before he defied his Superintendent and continued the investigation. "Did you kill Fred Chadwick?"

"You know I didn't."

It was enough. Deschanel was right. "Tell me again about the comedian."

Chapter 24

Devastating Loss

"Why are we questioning the comedian?" Walsh asked.

Marcus was angry enough with Walsh without his constable second-guessing his decisions. "We've been remiss in not bringing him in before now."

Walsh pouted. "I understood he's not been at *The Hippodrome* long, so what motive could he possibly have? Besides, we have the murderer in custody."

Marcus filled his lungs. He was expected to turn the constable into a good detective, but the task loomed like an uphill battle. "In time, you'll learn not to make hasty judgments. What evidence do we have against Deschanel? What's his motive for killing Chadwick?"

"He and the victim fought over Mrs. Chadwick," Walsh replied.

"If we charged everyone who'd ever fought with Fred Chadwick, the cells would be overflowing."

"But ..."

"Do you honestly believe a wealthy man who operates a luxury store would risk it all by killing someone?"

"But he's French."

Eyeing his assistant skeptically, Marcus shook his head. "That's your proof?" he asked, saddened that the young man harbored too many prejudices. "Bring Swales in."

A few minutes later, the comedian entered with Walsh.

Over the years, Marcus had acquired a sort of sixth sense about people. His first impressions weren't often wrong. It bothered him that he couldn't read Swales at all. The man didn't smile, nor frown. Nor did he seem nervous.

Apparently still smarting from the rebuke, Walsh nigh on shoved Swales into the chair across the table from Marcus. "State your full name and occupation," he growled.

"Kenneth Horatio Swales, Farmer."

Marcus raised an eyebrow. "Farmer? I understood you're the comedian at *The Hippodrome*."

"That's just temporary. Lean harvests the last few years forced me to look fer work in town."

"Why did Fred Chadwick take you on if you're not a comedian?"

"Dunno. In a bind I s'pose. T'other feller popped his clogs, sudden like."

"So, you don't intend to carry on at the theater for long?"

"Nay, 'tis country livin' suits me best."

"You hope to return to Blackrod soon, then?"

For the first time, doubt flickered in Swales' eyes. "Er ... aye. If 'tis all reet wi' the poleece now tha's arrested the killer."

Marcus had no real reason to prevent the man leaving town, but ... "I prefer everyone stay in Bolton for the moment."

"One more thing," he said as Swales got up to leave. "Do you have family in Blackrod? A wife perhaps."

There it was again. That tell-tale flicker—anger perhaps—that warned Marcus to be wary of the answer.

"Nay. On me own."

Marcus had loved a woman and lost her. The pain in Swales' response echoed his own grief.

MAGGIE DOUBTED Ken Swales had it in him to murder anyone. Still, something about him niggled at her. He was the only performer who hadn't worked at the theater for years and had turned up out of the blue at the very moment *The Hippodrome* needed a comedian. Fred had hired him despite the fact he had no talent for the job.

Upon arrival at the theater, she decided to seek out Goliath. It was possible the strongman had known Swales in Blackrod. It was a small farming and mining community but, from what Maggie understood, the farms were often miles away from each other. As a life-long townie, she had no experience of such a place. In town, working people lived in cramped, sometimes squalid accommodation, but often avoided familiarity with their neighbors. It was only out of necessity that women gathered in the street to do laundry at the standpipes.

She found Goliath in the storage room helping Maria load up her tray. Fred had kept strict control of the key, but Maggie had handed it over to Maria. She'd found it on a key ring with a bunch of others in his office. As expected, she'd managed to use them to lock and unlock the front and rear doors of the theater, and various storage cupboards. However, she still had to discover what two of the mystery keys opened. Perhaps it was better she not find out.

"Mrs. Chadwick," Goliath said nervously. "We were just ..."

"It's all right," she replied. "I trust you to manage the supply of cartons."

His shoulders relaxed. "Can we help tha wi' summat?"

Maggie hesitated. She didn't want to sound too inquisitive about Swales, but Goliath was the only person who could possibly help. "I've been thinking about our comedian."

"Aye," Goliath replied with a grin. "Nobody would blame tha for givin' him the 'eave-'o. But 'tis nay wunder 'e's such a sad sack."

Maggie was puzzled. "I'm not sure what you mean."

"Lost 'is betrothed."

Maggie hadn't expected this revelation. "He was engaged and the woman left him?"

"In a manner o' speakin'. Went doolally after she were raped by some bloke. Eventually drowned 'erself."

Maria gasped and Maggie too was horrified that Swales had suffered such a devastating loss, but a terrible premonition nagged at her. "Did Swales learn the rapist's identity?"

"Nay. The lass claimed she didn't know 'im. Some feller just passin' through, we reckon."

Breathless, her emotions in turmoil, Maggie hurried back to her dressing room. She didn't know if Fred had ever been to Blackrod, but had no doubt he was capable of rape. Her husband would see nothing wrong in forcing a woman against her will.

It was imperative she pass this new information on to Inspector Halliwell.

EMERSON DEAN DISDAINED GOSSIP, but couldn't resist listening in when he overheard Goliath and Maggie discussing Ken Swales. It seemed the comedian's fiancée had done away with herself after being raped. That was a tragedy—no wonder the man was so down in the dumps all the time. However, it was interesting that Maggie Chadwick had been enquiring about Swales. That likely meant she was planning to sack him—none too soon, in Emerson's opinion.

If that news was to somehow reach the ears of the other performers, they'd have somebody else to gossip about besides Emerson and his stylish hair.

Chapter 25

Despair

After only two days, Edouard feared he might go mad if he had to spend much more of his life cooped up in a cell. The Inspector was his only visitor. "Mrs. Chadwick asked to visit you," Halliwell told him. "Permission was denied."

The news only added to Edouard's frustration. On the one hand, he didn't want Maggie anywhere near the stinking cells, but, if he could hold her against him for a few brief minutes, he might feel more optimistic.

"Mr. Foster Marsh left a message that he had contacted the people at *Bon Marché* and told them of your arrest."

"He's the manager of the *Shangri-La,*" Edouard explained. "Good of him to think of doing that, though I wish he hadn't bothered them. Surely I'll be out of here soon."

"Well, Mrs. Chadwick did bring some information about the theater's comedian, but I don't know that it will help."

"But you have no evidence to convict me."

"You and I know that, but, to be honest, a jury doesn't always make its decision based on evidence."

Edouard shook his head. "You know I'm not guilty."

"But I won't be on the jury."

Terrified by the implications, but heartened that the Inspector believed him innocent, Edouard had to think of Maggie. "You must protect Mrs. Chadwick. She might put herself in danger if she pursues the real killer."

"I'll see what I can do, but the Superintendent is convinced we've charged the murderer. I've been reassigned to a case at the local brewery."

Edouard felt more alone and pessimistic after the policeman's departure. Maggie was his one hope, but contemplating the danger she might face tore him apart.

The next day, his despair deepened when a portly barrister hired by his sponsors at *Bon Marché* advised him to plead guilty. "Spare everyone the agony of drawing things out," he said condescendingly.

Maggie's despair grew by leaps and bounds after she received a visit from Mr. Sprague, a barrister hired to defend Edouard. He made it clear he disagreed with Edouard's decision to plead not guilty. "But he is innocent," she protested.

"The jury will find him guilty simply because the police have charged him," Sprague countered.

"Surely he won't go to trial if there is no evidence he was the killer. He had no motive."

"You're his motive, dear lady."

Maggie hated the patronizing tone of his remark, but, unfortunately, she could understand how a jury would interpret their liaison. "I suppose it doesn't count that I only met Mr. Deschanel the day before the murder."

"The prosecution will argue that he was enamored of you for a long time before that."

Sprague's visit was upsetting to say the least, but it strengthened Maggie's resolve to pursue the possibility that Swales was the murderer. If the prosecution was going to use her to persuade the jury of Edouard's guilt, she had to be the one to prove him innocent. But how to establish if her husband had ever been to Blackrod?

OVER THE YEARS, Rajendra Bandi had accumulated a goodly sum of money from his various businesses. Halliwell hadn't bothered to ask him if he had more cash stashed away elsewhere. He wasn't without powerful friends in the Indian community, many of whom would be anxious for him to keep their secrets. He sent messages to three of them, eventually receiving word he was to be freed pending his trial. The promise of monetary compensation in return for Rajendra's discretion had convinced Shiva Patel to provide guarantees that Rajendra would stay in town and be strictly supervised.

He wasn't certain what he would do once he was temporarily free. Any attempt to reestablish an opium den would be foolhardy. Halliwell had informed him that two of the addicts from the cellar had died, so he was skating on thin ice as it was. In any case, he'd lost his "partner in crime". Fred Chadwick used to arrange for the opium to be shipped to Liverpool and they traveled together to pick it up. Rajendra wouldn't miss those journeys with Chadwick. The man felt it necessary to impose himself on every woman he met. Rajendra disdained white women—they lacked the elegance and skill of women of his own race. He'd tried to convince Chadwick of the delights of peeling a silk sari off a willing woman—to no avail. The bigot didn't mince words when it came to dismissing *dirty* Indian women.

Alas, the matter of securing opium would have to wait until

after the trial. A few greased palms would ensure a light sentence in the unlucky event he were found guilty.

Informing the murderer he knew his identity was risky, but he could tell Mrs. Chadwick—in return for compensation, of course. She was likely desperate for any news that might prove her lover innocent, and might even be amenable to letting him rent the cellar again. He'd invested time and money making the dank place suitable for his businesses.

That reminded him of the boxes stored in *The Hippodrome's* cellar. Retrieving the junk might be worthwhile. At least then the fiasco wouldn't be a total loss.

MAGGIE HAD WALKED HOME from the theater alone many times. However, when she was the opening act, it was early evening when she left and lots of people were still out and about on the streets. Now, she was last on the bill and it was pitch dark when she left. She'd felt safe walking with Edouard. The circumstances of his absence made the lonely walk even more nerve-wracking.

Preoccupied with the dilemma of how to prove Edouard innocent in the event he was found guilty by a court, she squealed when a figure loomed out of the darkness and barred her path.

"Don't worry," he said, bowing low. "Rajendra Bandi at tha' service, Mrs. Chadwick."

"What?" was all she could manage from her parched throat. She was too far from home to make a run for it.

"I was Fred's partner. I mean tha no 'arm."

It came to her that this was the odious little man who ran the opium den in the cellar. "I thought you were in jail," she said.

"Out on a guarantee. I've information that might be of use."

She knew Bandi had seen a man in the theater the night of the murder and that Halliwell was aware of it. "You've already told the police what you know, haven't you?"

His eyes glowed, but it was too dark to see his face clearly. She had a feeling he was smirking. "I recognized the killer."

The urge to rip out his eyes was powerful. He wouldn't have approached her if he knew Edouard was the murderer, but, evidently, he hadn't told the police. The man she loved was languishing in prison and possibly about to be put on trial thanks to this ne'er-do-well's silence. Desperate to keep her voice under control, she replied, "And are you going to tell me who it is?"

"Fer a price."

Maggie's brain worked feverishly to come up with a solution to this dilemma. She needed the information he offered, but the prospect of paying him stuck in her craw. "I'll think of a suitable reward if you confirm my suspicions. You see, I've already figured out who the true culprit is."

She was pleased with herself when he hesitated, apparently taken by surprise. "Well?" she insisted. "Who was it?"

Chapter 26

Farce

Edouard had no appetite for the unpalatable gruel served by the guards at midday. Summarily informed he was being transferred that very afternoon, he wished he'd eaten something. Hunger fled when he was told his trial had been set for the next day at the Manchester Assizes.

"Trial?" he asked the guard who handcuffed him. "But I'm innocent. You have no evidence."

"They all say that. Get a move on. The Black Maria's waitin'."

Outside he was shoved into a black carriage along with several other men. The seats had been removed, so he sat on the floor, unable to understand a word spoken by the other garrulous prisoners who all turned out to be Irish.

For the first time, he felt the hope of a happy life with Maggie slipping away.

~

Despite being refused permission to visit Edouard's cell, Maggie turned up to the police station early every morning to repeat her request. Edouard's faithful driver, Albert, had placed himself and the carriage at Maggie's disposal which made getting about the town easier.

Her heart lurched when she was informed Edouard had been transferred to the Manchester Assizes where his trial was slated to begin that very day.

She hurried out of the station. Told of this latest development, Albert helped her board the carriage and they set off for Manchester.

Two harrowing hours later, they came to a halt outside the courthouse.

"There's a crowd goin' in just now," he told her. "Mayhap we're in time."

Her courage suddenly deserted her. Her trembling legs refused to move. What if Edouard didn't want her there? She couldn't bear to see him defeated.

She startled when the door opened.

"Ready?" Albert asked, extending his hand.

Shoving aside her silly fears, she accepted his help and marched into the building. Edouard would expect no less. Assuming the crowd of strangers had come out of morbid curiosity to see a murder trial, she followed them into a large courtroom, relieved she was able to push her way into a spot in the front row of the gallery.

The dark paneling of the high-ceilinged room was soberly intimidating. She espied a group of men she assumed were the members of the jury and prayed they were intelligent and would realize there was no evidence to convict Edouard.

She grimaced when she realized one of the bewigged gentlemen shuffling papers in the benches was none other than Sprague.

The hubbub ceased immediately and everyone rose when

the judge entered and took his seat high above the benches. "Bring in the prisoner," he intoned.

Clutching the railing, she heard footsteps on stone. She smiled her encouragement when Edouard appeared in the dock, though her heart was breaking. He looked pale and haggard but at least he returned the smile.

THE SUPERINTENDENT INFORMED Marcus that Deschanel had been transferred to Manchester where he was to be tried at the Assizes. "You're expected to give testimony for the prosecution," he was told.

Marcus hated the dirty city of Manchester and the prospect of helping to convict an innocent man made him sick to his stomach. Nevertheless, he took the train from Great Moor Street station, hailed a hack to take him from the railway station across town and presented himself at the courthouse, Walsh's notebook in his pocket.

Espying a familiar carriage outside the courthouse, he assumed Maggie had come in her lover's vehicle.

Led into the waiting room, he expected to be one of several witnesses waiting to give testimony but discovered he was alone. It seemed Deschanel's fate rested on his shoulders, a burden that tightened the knot of dread in his gut.

Called almost immediately to the witness box, he scanned the room while waiting for the clerk to administer the oath. Deschanel wore his own clothes, but he looked haggard. Pale and anxious, Maggie sat in the front row of the gallery amid strangers who'd likely come out of morbid curiosity. The hope in her gaze when she nodded to him tore at Marcus' heart.

The jury consisted of men who had the air of prosperity

about them—local landed gentry perhaps—which didn't augur well for a shopkeeper.

Marcus swore to tell the truth, then identified himself.

The prosecuting barrister began the questioning. "Are you the officer who arrested and charged the accused?"

"I am, but ..."

"Is it your understanding that Mr. Deschanel and the victim's wife are lovers?"

"I believe they are now, but ..."

"Is it true Mr. Deschanel was once arrested for viciously beating his father?"

Marcus felt sick. The notebook was in his pocket so how could the prosecution know of its contents? "Er ... yes, but ..."

"And was he also charged with the murder of his wife in Paris?"

Shaking with frustration, Marcus realized that nothing he could say would redeem Edouard Deschanel. "Yes, it's true, but ..."

"No further questions, M'Lud."

Exasperated, Marcus expected to explain the lack of evidence when Deschanel's barrister began his questioning, but his hopes were dashed when the bewigged gentleman stuck his nose in the air and declined to question him. He had no choice but to step down when the judge indicated he should do so.

Seething, he remained in the courtroom while the judge instructed the jury. He was surprised anyone was still awake after the monotonous, mostly incomprehensible and patronizing monologue.

As the restless members of the jury filed out, he nodded in acknowledgement of Maggie Chadwick's indication they meet outside.

❧

"THAT WAS A FARCE," Maggie exclaimed when she and the Inspector were settled in Edouard's carriage outside the courthouse.

"I agree."

His words were of some consolation but they didn't assuage the dread that seemed to have paralyzed her whole body. She took deep breaths to calm her agitation so she could tell Halliwell the important news. "Ken Swales murdered my husband."

"I was beginning to suspect him, but you sound so sure."

"Bandi told me. He recognized Swales that night."

"Did you visit him in the cells?"

"No, he's been paroled pending the trial."

The Inspector scratched his head. "Unbelievable. Why didn't he tell me this?"

He'd politely removed his hat before they entered the carriage. Maggie had never noticed he had a thick crop of brown hair. Besides being very tall and broad shouldered, he was actually an attractive man. Surely such a handsome specimen must be married, but this wasn't the time for small talk. "He thought there'd be more profit in telling me."

"What did he want in return?"

"Two hundred pounds and continued use of the cellar. I told him the money was out of the question. He doesn't know you gave me his ill-gotten gains."

"And the cellar?"

"I agreed but I'm hoping he'll be in jail for a long while and won't have need of the cellar."

"It's good news. The problem is that a court won't consider Rajendra Bandi a reliable witness. We need proof and to find a motive."

"I was hoping to travel to Blackrod. Swales' fiancée was raped there and subsequently killed herself. I have a terrible feeling that Fred was the rapist."

"You've been busy, but I can't allow you to go alone. Walsh and I will accompany you."

~

"I HEAR BANDI HAS BEEN BAILED," an exasperated Marcus exclaimed when he returned to the station.

Walsh gritted his teeth, clearly as upset as Marcus. "Some foreign bloke paid a bond to guarantee his good behavior until the trial."

"Bandi couldn't behave himself if his life depended on it," Marcus quipped. "It's galling that a guilty man walks free while an innocent man languishes in jail and will likely be hanged for a crime he didn't commit."

"You mean Deschanel?" Walsh asked, his eyes wide.

"Exactly."

"What makes you think ...?"

"You know as well as I do that there is no evidence to support the charge against him. We haven't done our job properly."

His assertion seemed to sober Walsh. "I suppose you're right, sir," the constable admitted. "Perhaps I've been too hasty in my judgment."

Encouraged by this development, Marcus knew he had to track down the real killer, despite the Superintendent's insistence they had charged the murderer. However, he deemed it preferable not to reveal what Mrs. Chadwick had told him about Swales. Once he found the proof ...

"We must dive deeper into the circumstances that brought the so-called comedian to Bolton."

"Where shall we start?" Walsh asked.

"Ever been to Blackrod, Constable?"

WAITING NERVOUSLY for the verdict in a damp cell beneath the courthouse, Edouard didn't hold out much hope. He was surprised the fidgeting jury foreman hadn't leapt from his seat and declared a guilty verdict before the yawning jury had even been sent out to deliberate.

It wasn't the first time he'd faced death and despair, but he'd never been in love before. He'd thought that he and Maggie had a whole lifetime of love and happiness ahead of them, but it seemed that dream wasn't to be.

His worst fear was that he wouldn't be around to protect her from the real murderer.

Chapter 27

Getting Closer

"I'm grateful you've allowed me to accompany you," Mrs. Chadwick told Marcus.

"We'd have been obliged to travel to Blackrod on the constabulary's quadricycle," Walsh explained, much to Marcus' annoyance. He didn't want Maggie to think he'd invited her simply to take advantage of Deschanel's carriage.

"Goodness," she replied. "That seems a long way to go on such a contraption. I believe I saw it at Fred's funeral."

"Yes," Marcus replied. "It's quite the invention. I was glad Walsh here did most of the pedaling."

The constable thrust out his chest. "It's easy once you get the hang of it."

Marcus glared at Walsh when Mrs. Chadwick paled.

"Sorry," Walsh said. "Unfortunate turn of phrase."

Marcus felt a small measure of relief. His assistant had perhaps come to realize the cruel reality Mrs. Chadwick and her lover faced.

"That's all right," she replied. "I'm simply glad you're helping me prove Edouard's innocence."

On the outskirts of the village of Blackrod, they passed a

public house called the *Rooster and Hen*. "Wait," Mrs. Chadwick exclaimed. "I seem to recall my husband once mentioning an inn by that name when he returned from one of his frequent journeys to who knows where."

Walsh rapped on the roof with his billy club and the carriage came to a halt.

"Thank you," she told the driver when he came to help her alight. "You've been a loyal servant."

"I'd do anything to help clear Mr. Deschanel's name," Albert replied. "He's an honorable man."

His assertion only strengthened Marcus' belief that the Frenchman was innocent. "We shouldn't be long," he told the driver.

The entry of two uniformed policemen in the company of a beautiful woman brought conversation inside the crowded inn to a full stop. Marcus was used to such attention, but Walsh gritted his teeth.

"We're looking for information about a certain Ken Swales," Marcus informed the publican who was leaning against the bar.

"What of it?"

"We understand he's from these parts," Walsh said.

"Aye. Farms up at top end, at least he used ta."

"But not now?" Marcus asked.

"Gone to work at some fancy play'ouse in Bolton. Can't blame 'im, mind, after what 'appened to his missus."

A handful of men had gathered around to eavesdrop on the conversation. Marcus supposed his presence had sparked curiosity.

"Drownded 'erself," one elderly chap offered.

"Why would she do that?" Marcus asked, though he knew the answer. "Was she a troubled soul?"

"Nah," the publican retorted. "She were workin' 'ere fer me when summat terrible 'appened."

"Aye," another old codger said. "Sheila were a grand lass, but this posh bloke fra town stole 'er virtue and she ne'er got o'er the shame."

"Nor did Ken," the publican added.

"This man from town," Mrs. Chadwick asked. "Did any of you know him?"

"Nay. Just passin' through on their way back from Liverpool. 'Im and a darkie."

"An Indian?" Marcus asked.

"Aye. One o' them 'Indus. 'Eathens are bad fer business. I woulda chucked 'im out but the tall white bloke threatened to wreck the place."

"He weren't the sort to mess wi'," one of the regulars said.

Walsh bristled. "And nobody thought to report this assault to the police?"

"Listen, lad," the publican sneered. "Some said Sheila were too pretty fer 'er own good and musta led 'im on."

"Nay," came the chorus from shaking heads. "She didn't want any fuss. This is a small village."

"In any case, Ken swore he'd fix it."

Having heard enough, Marcus indicated they leave the inn. "Well," he said once they were settled in the carriage. "It's pretty clear Chadwick was the rapist and that Swales is the killer, but a good barrister will make short work of the testimony of a few yokels. We need absolute proof."

Tears brimming, Mrs. Chadwick inhaled deeply. "How do we achieve that, short of making Swales confess?"

"Jury's back," the court bailiff told Edouard. "Let's be havin' thee."

He was glad to leave the tiny cell, but his legs felt like lead as he mounted the stone steps to the dock.

One look at the scowling faces of the jury told him they'd found him guilty.

He barely heard the rest of the proceedings. As expected, he was to be hanged. It struck him as ironic. Like father, like son. "Maggie," he rasped, curling up on the bunk when he was returned to the cell.

EMERSON DEAN WAS FEELING QUITE optimistic. A distraught Maggie had told everyone at the theater that Deschanel had been found guilty and sentenced to be hanged. She assured them that she had uncovered evidence to prove him innocent, but Emerson supposed that was wishful thinking on her part. He'd give her a month to come to terms with her grief and then reveal his feelings. She'd be grateful for a shoulder to cry on.

He wondered if she still planned to sack the comedian. If Emerson let Swales know his days at *The Hippodrome* were numbered, he might leave of his own volition. Maggie would be grateful to be spared the unpleasant task of sacking him. Good riddance to bad rubbish. The man was no comedian.

He was taken by surprise when Swales approached him after Maggie's tearful announcement.

"What does she mean?" Swales asked. "New evidence?"

Emerson deemed it a curious question. "What does it matter to thee? Rumor has it tha'll soon be sacked."

"Why?"

Emerson didn't care for the belligerent tone of the question. Was it really necessary to point out that the man was hopeless at his job? "I'm sure Mrs. Chadwick will explain her decision later. She received the terrible news about Mr. Deschanel shortly after getting back from Blackrod, so she'll need time to compose herself."

Without warning, Swales fisted his hands in Emerson's freshly ironed waistcoat. "Why did she go to Blackrod?" he demanded, his nose inches from Emerson's.

"How should I know? Let go. You're ruining my uniform."

He staggered backwards when Swales shoved him and stalked away. "Well," he huffed. "Some people."

Chapter 28

A Lift On The Way

Maggie sat in her silent dressing room. Two of the chorus line girls had helped her dress for her performance. They smothered her with hugs and sympathy, but a fog of lethargy had settled in Maggie's brain, making it impossible to respond. She'd dreamt of a happy life with Edouard, but Fred's greedy sexual appetite had stolen the dream away. If he hadn't raped a young woman in Blackrod, Swales wouldn't have sought revenge. She'd rather have borne the continued misery of life with Fred than contemplate Edouard's execution.

The prospect of performing tonight churned her stomach, but the show had to go on, despite her exhaustion. People were depending on her for their livelihood. It was tempting to seek solace in a bottle of gin, but it was vital she keep her wits about her. Somehow, she had to find proof of the comedian's guilt.

Hearing the audience groan, she realized Swales was on stage and she was the next act. She shook herself out of her stupor and left the dressing room. Ignoring the comedian's scowl as they passed in the wings, she strutted onto the stage, head held high. The deafening applause constricted her throat. The common people's sympathy lay with her. They understood her torment.

She opened her mouth to begin the first song, but no sound emerged. Panic subsided when the audience belted out the lyrics. They carried her through most of her act, but she came close to surrendering to her grief when it came time to sing the last line of her favorite song. She was too choked to voice the words but the audience knew what she needed to hear.

Pray heaven may give us all a lift on the way.

Weeping, she took her bow and left the stage to raucous applause.

She briefly wondered in passing why Swales was still in the wings and still scowling. It wasn't until she reached the safety of her dressing room that reality punched her in the belly. Swales knew that she rightly suspected he was her husband's killer.

Marcus hadn't been to a music hall since before he'd joined the police force. Before her untimely death, he'd often taken Eliza to *The Hippodrome*. They could only afford to sit in the gallery, but they'd been young and in love. In those days, the theater had seemed grand, opulent even. It now looked tawdry and past its prime.

Maggie wasn't one of the turns then, of course, so he'd never seen her perform. He'd not expected her to appear tonight of all nights, but he'd come to make sure she was safe if she did turn up.

He sat in the gallery, for old times' sake, and had come in mufti so as to blend in. That thought made him chuckle. At more than six feet in height, he would never blend in.

The show was entertaining and he almost forgot his reason for being there until the comedian came on. He gritted his teeth, itching to get his hands on the murdering sod who intended to let another man hang for his crime. He could almost condone the wretch killing Chadwick, but be a man and own up to it when someone else is mistakenly found guilty of the crime.

He wasn't surprised the audience booed Swales off the stage, but Maggie's appearance took him aback. By the end of her moving performance, there wasn't a dry eye in the theater. Even Marcus had to blow his nose to keep from blubbering.

He sobered when, from his vantage point, he caught a glimpse of Swales skulking in the wings.

EDOUARD'S HOPE that he might see Maggie one last time if he were transferred back to Bolton was cruelly dashed when he was summarily informed his sentence would be carried out in Manchester. He had to let her know how much she meant to him and it seemed the only way to do that was to write a letter. He asked for and was given paper, pen and ink. The guards seemed more inclined to be obliging now he was a walking dead man.

He thought long and hard before committing his feelings to paper.

My darling Maggie,

I do not fear death. I only regret that I did not tell you how much I love you when I had the chance. Before this catastrophe befell us, I planned to ask for your hand in marriage. Would you have said yes? I will go to my grave believing you would, that you love me with all your heart.

Alas, our dream wasn't meant to be, but I want you to be happy. Do not weep too long for me. You will find happiness with another, but I'm confident you will never forget your Edouard.

Au revoir, Reine du music-hall et de mon coeur.

Je t'aime,
Edouard.

AT HIS REQUEST, a priest came to hear his confession. Sympathetic to the situation, the cleric agreed to ensure the letter was delivered to Maggie in a timely manner.

Chapter 29

Attack

Maggie dithered in her dressing room long after the show was over. Her flat wasn't far away, but she'd be vulnerable walking the dark streets alone. She needed an escort and, lamentably, she knew who would jump at the chance.

She found Emerson still tidying up in the hall. As expected, he quickly agreed to walk her home. Perhaps he was worried about her. She might have felt guilty leading him on, but better safe than sorry.

He retrieved his coat and politely offered his arm as they exited the rear door. The smell of his pomaded hair was overwhelming and she wished he didn't feel the need to chatter on about inconsequential matters. Perhaps her continued failure to respond would eventually shut him up.

They had just turned into Bank Street when he fell strangely silent. By the time she realized he was no longer beside her, someone grabbed her. Panic surged when the attacker clamped his hands around her throat and she looked into the manic eyes of Ken Swales. She clawed at his hands, struggling to remove them, but he was too strong. Her legs buckled. She couldn't breathe and seemed fated to die within sight of her flat without ever telling Edouard how much she loved him. She was sinking into a black pit of despair.

Suddenly, the pressure was gone. She heaved air into her beleaguered lungs and collapsed into the arms of Inspector Marcus Halliwell.

~

WHEN MARCUS SAW Maggie and Emerson Dean leave the theater, he thought perhaps there was no necessity for him to follow. He said a silent prayer of thanks that his instincts had convinced him otherwise. After blowing his whistle to summon help, he held Maggie tightly as she gasped for breath. Her struggle reminded him keenly of Eliza's last days. He'd been unable to save the woman he loved, but he'd been in time to save Maggie Chadwick.

Curled up on the ground, Dean groaned.

Two constables arrived at the run and took hold of the waiter who was by now trying to stand.

"Not him," Marcus shouted impatiently. "The attacker got away, down Bank Street."

They dropped Dean and ran off down the hill, whistles trilling.

"It was Swales," Maggie rasped, gripping the sleeve of Marcus' coat like a shipwreck survivor clings to driftwood.

"Good grief," Dean exclaimed, holding his head as he staggered to his feet. "I told him you were going to sack him but I never imagined he'd do something like this."

Marcus gritted his teeth. If they caught Swales, Dean's bungling interference would provide him with an excuse for attacking Maggie. He'd be charged with assault, not murder.

~

"No need to come up the stairs to my flat," Maggie told Halliwell. "I'll be safe now, thanks to you."

When they encountered a man sitting on the top step, she was glad he'd shaken his head and escorted her all the way to the door.

"Who are you and what do you want?" the Inspector demanded.

Maggie saw the "dog collar" when the man stood, alarm in his gaze. She didn't blame him. He had no way of knowing the giant who accosted him was a policeman.

"I'm Father Paderborn, and I've a letter for Mrs. Chadwick, sent through a fellow priest in Manchester."

"Edouard," she breathed, accepting the letter with trembling hands.

"My thanks, Father," Halliwell said.

"Will they catch Swales?" she asked after the priest hurried down the stairs.

"Hopefully, and I'll speak to the Superintendent at the earliest opportunity. We must stop the execution. Lock the door."

Safely inside, she unfolded the letter and held it to her nose, hoping to catch a faint trace of the man she'd loved and lost. She read the contents over and over, crying until she could cry no more. Exhausted, she fell asleep fully clothed, clutching the missive to her breast.

~

Shortly after dawn, Marcus attended the Bolton Borough police station, surprised to almost bump into the Superintendent.

"Halliwell! Good! We've been waiting for your account so we can formally charge this comedian fellow."

Marcus' spirits rose. He'd joined in the unsuccessful pursuit until well after midnight. "They caught him?"

"Yes. He's in the cells. Claims he just meant to scare Mrs. Chadwick, angry because he'd heard she was going to sack him. He's very repentant. He's been through a lot, you know, what with his fiancée dying so tragically. The threat of losing his job was the last straw, I suppose."

Marcus resisted the urge to roll his eyes. He had to remember he was dealing with an idiot. "Sir," he began. "Given the circumstances, do you not feel it prudent to postpone Mr. Deschanel's hanging?"

"For what reason? A jury found him guilty."

"With all due respect, the jury did not know that Fred Chadwick may have raped Swales' fiancée, thus giving Maggie's attacker a motive for murder. I believe he intended to kill Mrs. Chadwick because she was getting close to the truth."

"All sounds rather tenuous to me," his superior muttered. "And how do you know all this? Aren't you supposed to be dealing with a murder at the brewery?"

Marcus realized he risked angering the Superintendent who believed the murder case was closed, but he had to speak. "Tenuous or not, sir, do you want to be blamed for hanging the wrong man?"

Doubt flickered in narrowed eyes. "Indeed not. I'll send word to Manchester. But you need to bring me proof Swales is the killer."

Chapter 30

Little Black Book

Edouard slept fitfully, often waking up in the middle of the night drenched in sweat. He was given no opportunity to bathe. No doubt it was deemed a waste of effort for a condemned man to be clean. He'd always been fastidious about cleanliness. Death would at least release him from the indignity of an unwashed body.

Even during the interminably long days, he dreamt of Maggie, of holding her, of tasting her juices. The resulting arousals had to be dealt with. He'd never had to resort to such measures and was deeply ashamed of his inability to control his needs and emotions.

His gut clenched one morning when the cell door clanged open unexpectedly. Dawn hadn't yet crept into the cell. Was today the day?

He was still trembling after the guard informed him there'd been a stay of execution pending further inquiries. He gulped air in an effort to slow his racing heart.

Left alone in the dark, he fell to his knees, made the sign of his Savior, and tearfully thanked God for Maggie's courage and determination.

Lost in thought as she sipped her morning coffee, Maggie tensed when someone tapped at the door. It couldn't be Swales. Marcus had come to tell her the comedian was locked up and that Edouard's execution had been stayed—for the moment. She wanted to kiss the tall policeman, until he cautioned that they still needed irrefutable evidence. The wretch's claim he'd only meant to frighten her stuck in her craw. She would never forget the murderous intent in those manic eyes.

Tempted to ignore the person at the door, she crept closer. "Who is it?" she finally asked.

"My name is Arthur Bootle. I'm a solicitor from Bootle, Bootle and Spank."

"I don't need a solicitor," she replied, stifling the urge to titter at the name of his firm. Surely this was some ruse?

"You misunderstand. I was your late husband's solicitor."

Fred had a solicitor? Her husband probably owed him money.

"What do you want with me?"

"Your husband left a will. Our offices are in Liverpool, so I've only recently become aware of his death."

A will? She could scarcely believe Fred would bother with such a thing. Nevertheless, opening the door as far as the safety chain would allow revealed a little man in an expensive suit and bowler hat who couldn't be anything but a solicitor. The pince-nez perched halfway down his nose was the final touch that convinced her he was harmless.

"Come in," she said, opening the door.

"First of all," he said, making straight for one of the kitchen chairs without so much as a by-your-leave. "My sincere condolences. I see you're still not over the shock."

She didn't bother to explain the red-rimmed eyes were caused by tears for Edouard, not Fred.

Tsking sympathetically, he withdrew papers from a large satchel. "Here we are," he said, squinting over the top of his pince-nez. "You're the sole beneficiary of all Mr. Chadwick's assets, including his bank accounts at the Westminster and the deed to a place called *The Hippodrome*. I assume it's a theater and that you know where it is."

"Yes," she replied, still gobsmacked by the news Fred had bank accounts.

"And this," he exclaimed, holding out a small metal cashbox. "I have one key, dear lady, and I trust you have the other."

Confused, Maggie shook her head, until she remembered the mystery keys from Fred's office. Where on earth had she put them?

~

MARCUS ACKNOWLEDGED he was neglecting the mystery of the body found floating in a vat of ale at Longworth's brewery, but he couldn't get his mind off the murder of Fred Chadwick. He'd racked his brain for a way to prove Swales guilty. He'd even considered sending Walsh to beat a confession out of the wretch.

He was about to take another shot at convincing the Superintendent of Deschanel's innocence when Maggie Chadwick hurried into the cupboard that served as his office. Red in the face and clearly excited, she thrust a cashbox onto the pile of papers on his desk. "Wait until you see this," she exclaimed.

A dapper little fellow in a bowler hat tried to squeeze into the tiny space. "The box was in my safekeeping, you see ..."

"Yes, yes," Maggie interrupted, opening the lid. "I'll explain all that. It's the contents that are important."

She took out a small, black notebook. "Apparently proud of his dastardly deeds, my monster of a husband kept a record of his conquests."

Marcus was intrigued. "Are you saying …?"

"Yes," she replied, leafing through the pages. "Here it is. *Sheila, barmaid at the Rooster and Hen, Blackrod. Tasty virgin. Easy prey.*"

Trembling and ashamed, she passed the book to Marcus. "You'll see he's even stuck a lock of the poor girl's hair to the page. Same with the other ten women he gleefully raped."

Marcus examined the pages of the book, sickened to his stomach by the cad's boastful comments about the innocent women he'd violated. Then he met Maggie's enquiring gaze. "Got him!" he declared with a smile. "Wait here."

Disappointed to have been rearrested for accosting Mrs. Chadwick—a misunderstanding at the very least—Rajendra was startled out of the first good sleep he'd had in a while. He was all set to swear at the guard who'd disturbed him—until he looked into the angry face of Inspector Halliwell and saw the small, black book thrust under his nose.

"You knew," Halliwell hissed. "And did nothing to stop him."

Rajendra shrugged. "Men will be men, tha knows."

"Don't give me that, and don't tell me the women asked for it."

Rajendra searched for a way out of this coil. "Fred Chadwick weren't a man to cross."

"Well, he paid for his crimes. I'm going to make sure you're sent away for life—unless you come with me to the Superintendent's office and testify it was Swales you saw in the theater the night Chadwick was killed."

"If I tell thee, it'll count in my favor?"

"I make no promises, but I'll see what I can do."

"Lead on, then."

Chapter 31

Reunited

Left alone in the Inspector's tiny office with only Arthur Bootle for company, Maggie searched for some topic of conversation but found none. It was as if every fiber of her being was focused on being told Edouard would be freed. Her brain couldn't concentrate on anything else.

"I had no idea what was in the box," Bootle eventually told her.

"How could anyone know or even imagine what it contained?" she replied.

"I expected more keepsakes, like the miniature."

Maggie didn't know how to respond. Fred had kept a miniature portrait of his mother in the box with the vile diary, hard to fathom since he'd never had a good word to say about his mother. Maggie vaguely remembered Freda Chadwick as a stern, God-fearing woman. "His mother must be turning in her grave," was all she could think to say.

She stood quickly when Halliwell returned with another, older policeman whose furrowed brow didn't augur well. Fearing she might swoon as the room tilted, she gripped Bootle's arm.

"Mrs. Chadwick, I'm Superintendent Borthwick. In view of the latest developments, I've sent word to Manchester that Mr. Deschanel is not guilty of the crime of murder."

Elated, Maggie was nevertheless annoyed when no apology seemed to be forthcoming. Halliwell had told her it was the Superintendent who had pushed for Edouard to be charged, despite the lack of evidence. Drawing on the courage that had sustained her through the difficult years with Fred, she narrowed her eyes. "Had Inspector Halliwell not done a thorough job of investigating my husband's murder, you'd have hanged an innocent man." She nodded at Bootle. "I plan to speak to my solicitor about your conduct."

"Indeed," Bootle declared. "Reprehensible."

And with that, he escorted her out of the police station.

EDOUARD WAS TRYING to convince himself to eat the stale bread roll he'd been given for breakfast when he received an unexpected visitor. He hadn't seen his barrister since the trial and had a few choice words to fling at Sprague. If only he knew the English equivalents!

"Deschanel," the barrister muttered, as if they were old acquaintances.

"What do you want?" Edouard growled.

"Now, is that any way to speak to the man who has come to tell you you're free to go?"

The urge to punch the pompous bastard's nose was powerful, but he couldn't jeopardize his freedom. Sprague would get his comeuppance when Edouard gave an accounting of the barrister's poor performance to the owners of *Bon Marché* who were paying his bill. "Free?" he echoed.

"Another man has been charged. An eye witness has come

forward and there's some damning evidence to convict. The guard outside has your clothes. Good luck."

As Sprague strutted out, the guard entered bearing a pile of Edouard's own clothes. He deposited the garments on the bunk then lingered in the cell until Edouard asked, "Want to watch me strip off?"

Left alone, he quickly removed the hated prison overalls, spread his arms wide, inhaled deeply and savored the moment of being naked ... and free.

Normally, he wouldn't think of putting clothes on in his present state, but needs must. Feeling more confident in his own clothing, he sauntered out of the cell then realized he had no idea how to get out of the cells beneath the courtroom.

He bristled when another man approached and reached for his hand. "I just heard the news," he said. "I came to apologize most sincerely."

Edouard was grateful that at least someone had come to apologize, but who was this man?

"You don't recognize me without my wig. I'm the prosecuting barrister."

Of course!

Edouard couldn't see the point of blaming this man for his misfortune. "You were just doing your job, unlike my barrister."

"Indeed! Well, I'm certain you want to get out of his place. Let me show you the way."

They soon emerged into the street. The air smelled of smoke and industry. But it was the smell of *liberté* and Edouard filled his lungs, vowing never again to take his freedom for granted.

"Do you need a lift?" the barrister asked.

Edouard was reminded of Maggie's song. *A lift along the way.*

"No, thank you. Mrs. Chadwick will be here to take me home."

~

EDOUARD'S DRIVER had pushed the horse hard. Albert was just as anxious as Maggie to retrieve his boss from the Assizes, so she didn't need to encourage him.

Her heart surged into her throat when she saw Edouard standing outside the courthouse. "There he is," she exclaimed to Arthur Bootle, who had insisted on accompanying her.

The man she loved grinned when he saw the carriage and was waiting with open arms to catch her as she leapt from the vehicle.

"Maggie," he breathed, lifting her off her feet and twirling her around.

"Edouard," she replied, dizzy with happiness as she savored the warmth of his embrace.

"I'm afraid I stink of the jail," he lamented.

She inhaled deeply. "You smell wonderful to me. Kiss me."

His lips met hers. She poured all her pent-up fear and longing into returning his kiss. She tasted again his unique flavor when their tongues mated, and relished the silky smoothness of the dark beard she'd never seen before.

She suckled his thrusting tongue, needing to draw it further into her mouth, to let him know she understood his need and wanted all of him.

Albert's loud whistling broke them apart. Edouard embraced his faithful employee. Her heart melted when he then smiled at her, his eyes full of love.

"The answer's yes, by the way," she said, feeling the heat of embarrassment rise in her face.

"Yes?" he queried.

"Yes, I will marry you."

"Wait," he exclaimed, going down on one knee. "We're going to do this properly. Maggie Chadwick, will you do me the very great honor of becoming my wife?"

She took hold of his hand and pulled him to his feet. "*Oui*, Edouard Deschanel. I can't wait to marry my sexy Frenchman."

Slow applause drew their attention. She'd forgotten about the solicitor. "Edouard, Arthur Bootle was my husband's solicitor. It was he who brought us the final proof we needed to convict Swales. I'll explain later."

Edouard kept an arm around Maggie's waist as he proffered his hand. "You have my eternal thanks, *Monsieur* Bootle."

"Very happy to have been of assistance," Bootle replied, accepting the handshake.

Chapter 32

A Bath Beckons

The trio boarded the carriage.

En route, Maggie explained the role Arthur Bootle had played in bringing the good news about the will and the lockbox. She dreaded telling him about the diary.

"So, you personally represented Mr. Chadwick?" Edouard asked.

"Yes, I'm the junior partner of Bootle, Bootle and Spank. My father is the other Bootle."

"Your father is the senior partner?"

Bootle gripped his knees. "Er ... no."

"Yet, your name comes first. In France the senior partner's name would be first."

Bootle shifted his weight, clearly uncomfortable. "Yes, well, Mr. Spank is the senior partner, but my father and I convinced him that Spank, Bootle and Bootle sounded ... well ... not quite the thing."

"I see," Edouard replied, winking at Maggie.

She was glad of the respite before having to explain about the vile record of Fred's crimes.

Edouard sat in silence for a long while after she described

the diary's contents. Then, he took her hand, raised it to his lips and said, "My darling Maggie, I swear I will do everything in my power to erase Fred's treachery from your memory."

He meant what he said, but, in truth, Maggie didn't want to forget completely. Her husband's perfidy would be a constant reminder of how fortunate she was to have met Edouard Deschanel.

~

BOOTLE MADE it abundantly clear he'd be more than willing to represent Maggie's interests. Edouard got the feeling the money in Fred's bank accounts amounted to a sizable sum. Maggie was now a rich woman, yet she still loved her shopkeeper, and he'd be eternally grateful for her generous heart.

He offered to transport Bootle all the way back to Liverpool, but the solicitor explained he had traveled to Bolton in his own carriage. They dropped him off at *The Pack Horse* hotel in the town center from whence Edouard directed his driver to take them to the front doors of *Shangri-La*.

"Should we not be more discreet?" she asked when the vehicle came to a halt.

"We have nothing to be ashamed of," he replied. "People have to see that we are only guilty of loving each other."

"You place a lot of faith in your fellow man."

Edouard acknowledged inwardly that she was right, but he didn't intend to spend his life avoiding the public. His hope that Lancashire folks would sympathize with their trials and tribulations was borne out when he and Maggie entered the store hand in hand and received a hearty welcome. Employees and customers alike applauded and cheered. The news of Swales' arrest and Edouard's acquittal had apparently spread fast.

Foster emerged from the crowd of well-wishers. "Welcome

home, Sir," his manager said, shaking his hand and bowing to Maggie. "Mrs. Chadwick."

"Thank you," she replied graciously, smiling with obvious relief.

"Maggie and I plan to marry at the earliest opportunity," Edouard told Foster. "However, right now, I intend to go to my apartment and soak in a hot bath."

"Of course," Foster replied with a knowing smile. "I'll arrange for hot water. Would you like me to send refreshments from the café?"

"In about an hour," Edouard replied, estimating how long he planned to *relax* in the bathtub with Maggie.

Upon entering the apartment, Edouard flopped down wearily on the settee and lifted one foot. "I hate to ask this," he said. "Can I trouble you to help me ease off my boots?"

"Of course," she replied, fully sympathetic to his exhaustion.

She straddled his outstretched leg, grasped the boot and tugged. It took some effort, but she eventually succeeded in removing the footwear. She was about to embark on the second boot when a soft tap at the door heralded a team of lads carrying pails of steaming water.

Discreetly ignoring her and Edouard, they proceeded to the water closet, poured out the water, then left.

By the time she got the second stubborn boot off, this scene had played itself out three times.

"At last," Edouard groaned as she sat beside him.

"Would you like me to massage your feet?" she asked, thinking he was referring to the removal of his boots.

"Hmm," he replied. "It's tempting. I thought I might go mad

watching your wiggling *derrière* when you were wrestling with my boots. However, I was anticipating a massage of another part of my body while we bathe."

On previous visits, Maggie had seen the enormous bathtub in Edouard's apartment. A woman in love couldn't help but fantasize about sharing such a tub with her lover. Now, it seemed her fantasy was about to come true. "Together?" she asked, realizing immediately how silly the question sounded.

"Are you suddenly shy with your Edouard?" he teased.

She had promised herself always to be honest with this darling man. "No, I long to see my exotic lover naked again."

He stood abruptly and pulled her to her feet. "Your wish is my command. Come."

EDOUARD EYED THE BECKONING TUB, hesitant to remove his clothes lest Maggie see the last of the bruises from Walsh's beating. He'd imagined bathing with her at least a hundred times, but he'd never anticipated he'd be doing it with a bruised body in dire need of a good scrub.

"Let me help," she said, easing the coat off his shoulders.

His tension eased as she helped him remove his shirt. This remarkable woman knew him better than he knew himself. She stiffened when she saw the bruises. "Who did this?" she asked, kissing away his pain.

"It doesn't matter now," he replied, shoving down his trousers, then his drawers.

She smiled, her gaze fixed on his arousal.

Uncharacteristically nervous, he put a foot in the hot water. "I'll jump in first and scrub off the smell of the jail."

"Help me out of this dress first," she replied.

Moments later, they stared at each other's nakedness. The

urge to claim her immediately was powerful, but she deserved a sweet-smelling lover. He startled when she took his hand and helped him get into the tub.

"Let's pretend," she cooed, eyes full of mischief. "You're my medieval knight and I'm the dutiful wife who's going to cleanse away the sweat of the joust."

As he sank into the blessedly hot water, his cock agreed wholeheartedly with her plan. "Cleanse away, Goodwife," he said, handing her the cake of soap.

Chapter 33

This Time

Keenly aware of her nakedness but happily comfortable being unclothed in the presence of this man, Maggie knelt by the side of the tub and stared at Edouard's well-muscled body, scarcely able to believe how readily he aroused her sexual interest.

Fred had been just as broad in the shoulders, his chest as chiseled, his face as handsome. Yet, even at the outset of their relationship, she'd never craved him as she craved Edouard. She'd grown to hate Fred, but knew in her heart she would never escape the alchemy that drew her to Edouard Deschanel.

She chuckled inwardly as she soaped up the washcloth. Alchemy! Medieval knights! What next? Love had stolen her wits and she thanked God for it. Life with Edouard would never be dull and fun had been a long time coming.

She washed his arms, then his armpits, delighting in the groans of pleasure her ministrations produced. His eyes flew open when she smoothed her soapy hands over his chest. There wasn't enough water in the tub to completely cover his growing arousal as she teased his male nipples. Feeling naughty, she announced, "Feet next, Sir Knight."

"I think not, saucy wench," he replied, hauling her into the tub.

A tidal wave of water spilled over onto the tiled floor.

His toe-curling kiss silenced her squealing laughter.

REVELING IN MAGGIE'S LAUGHTER, Edouard leaned back in the tub, positioned her on top of him, and nestled his arousal between her legs. He couldn't let another precious day go by without being inside her, but a bathtub wasn't the place for their first joining.

She buried her face in the crook of his neck and heaved a deep sigh, seemingly content, as he was, to be skin to skin, breasts to chest, belly to belly in the warm water.

He settled his hands on her *derrière*, chuckling when his hips inevitably responded to his cock's urging to thrust into her warm, wet sheath. He had to take his mind off his pressing need. "So, now you're a rich woman, will you still perform?"

She looked up at him, her eyes wide. "Of course. The stage has kept me sane for years. I'm safe there. The common people love me."

"I love you more and I'm your security now," he replied, slightly offended but understanding what she meant.

"I know I will always be able to rely on you, but will you object if I go on being Miss Maggie, at least as long as I am able?"

He pecked a kiss on her cheek. "I can't wait to brag that my wife is the redoubtable Miss Maggie, Queen of *The Hippodrome Music Hall*."

"Won't your wealthy clients censure you for it?"

"On the contrary. A bit of scandal can do wonders for business."

It came to him that the water had cooled. Gooseflesh marched across her cold *derrière*. "It's time," he whispered, lifting her off his body.

"I DON'T KNOW why I'm so nervous," Maggie admitted after Edouard patiently patted her dry. "I ache to belong to you."

Smiling, he led her to his bedroom where they lay side by side in the big bed, holding hands. "This is a momentous step forward in our relationship," he said softly. "I'm nervous too. I want our joining to be memorable for you."

"It will be," she reassured him, humbled by his regard for her feelings.

They turned to face each other. He nibbled her lower lip. When she thought he would coax open her mouth, he switched to her earlobes. Her nipples responded to the sound of his warm breath. She sifted her fingers through his hair and gently pulled his head back so his lips met hers again.

Kissing became more than she had ever hoped for. He cradled her face in his hands and entwined his fingers in her hair. He kissed the side of her neck, her forehead, her eyelids, her throat, her shoulder. He was worshipping a woman who'd never felt so wanton, so desirable.

He coaxed her lips with his tongue, then withdrew when she opened. "You're teasing me," she whispered.

He chuckled in reply—a deep, throaty chuckle that caused moisture to gush in a very intimate place.

Wise to his ploy, she captured his tongue before he could withdraw and sucked it into her mouth. She suckled him greedily then set him free. "You learn fast," he growled into her mouth, his words vibrating against her lips.

"I can't wait to have you inside me," she replied, her hips gyrating in the time-honored rhythm.

"Patience, *mon amante*," he whispered.

EDOUARD ADVISED PATIENCE, but doubted he could hold off much longer. The urge to penetrate Maggie was powerful, but he wanted her to release first. A happy, wet sheath would increase enjoyment for them both when he finally thrust inside. He had erotic plans for some private places, only hoping he could last long enough before claiming the prize he sought.

He began with her glorious breasts, squeezing a nipple before sucking it into his mouth. He suckled and teased with his tongue, elated by her moans of pleasure. She opened her legs, releasing the faint aroma of female arousal. He inhaled deeply, intensifying his desire as he turned his attention to laving the other nipple. He'd learned what she liked and had watched her need grow before, but this was different. This time ...

But he was getting ahead of himself. Patience, he scolded as he drew her to the edge of the bed and knelt on the carpeted floor. He lifted her hips and darted his tongue into her juices, filling his senses with the sweetness of pure honey and the taste of home. His cock saluted her scream when he suckled the diamond of her desire and she fell into the abyss.

He wasn't sure from where he found the control, but he couldn't deny himself one more secret pleasure. Back on his feet, he flipped her over and used his thumbs to part the cheeks of her *derrière*. The sight of a perfect pink rosette sent him tumbling over the edge. He covered her body and plunged into a warm, welcoming sheath. Hands clamped on her hips, he thrust and thrust like a man possessed until sperm catapulted from his body. Bliss became euphoria when she screamed her mutual fulfillment.

Chapter 34

Demons Exorcised

Swales' trial was scheduled for the day before his wedding, but Edouard was determined to attend. Maggie was reluctant but understood his need to exorcise the dark memories of the courthouse and face the true killer.

A jubilant Albert drove them to Manchester in the carriage.

Neither was expected to testify so they found seats in the gallery.

"Feels a bit different from up here," he quipped in an effort to calm his racing heart.

"I'll do whatever I can to help dispel the memories," Maggie replied, meshing her fingers with his.

He raised their joined hands to his lips. "I know."

Scanning the barristers and clerks milling about in the benches, he noted the same man who'd acted for the prosecution at his trial. Following his gaze, Maggie nodded. "At least he came to apologize," she whispered.

"Which is more than can be said for Sprague. "I've written an account of his performance to my sponsors."

Still holding hands, they stood along with everyone else

when the judge entered. Edouard was mildly surprised it was the same man who'd presided over his trial.

He steeled himself to control his anger when Swales was summoned, but felt only pity when the wretch appeared in the dock.

Maggie squeezed his hand, clearly sensing his over-whelming relief.

"You know me so well," he whispered close to her ear.

"I'm glad we came," she replied. "I can't find it in my heart to hate him."

Several witnesses were called, including Angus McCray, the landlord from the *Rooster and Hen* and even Rajendra Bandi. Inspector Halliwell was the main witness for the prosecution. Edouard owed the policeman a debt of gratitude for saving Maggie's life and for pursuing the case despite his superior's orders to the contrary.

By the time the jury was sent out to deliberate, Edouard was also glad he'd faced his demons. He would never forget this place nor the ordeal he'd undergone. He didn't believe in fate, but perhaps it had all been part of some master plan to bring him and Maggie together.

The jury returned a guilty verdict in less than half an hour. Before sentencing him to be hanged, the judge railed at Swales for almost allowing an innocent man to be executed in his stead. There was no reaction from the farmer turned comedian. Edouard felt heartily sorry for the wretch.

Maggie had admitted she would never forget the madness in her attacker's eyes. The disaster that had befallen Swales and his betrothed had obviously plunged the man into madness.

~

Called to testify at Swales' trial, Marcus entered the courtroom feeling much better than the last time he'd been summoned. He'd half expected Swales to plead guilty since he'd more or less confessed to the crime after being charged. It seemed the defense had persuaded him to plead innocence. Marcus wasn't concerned. He had enough evidence to convict.

Out of the corner of his eye, he espied Deschanel and Mrs. Chadwick up in the gallery. He was glad they'd come. Perhaps seeing justice done might erase the terrible memories. They deserved to be happy.

He breathed more easily when the guilty verdict was given. The judge's scolding was reminiscent of the one another judge gave Bandi at his trial for not disclosing a killer's identity sooner. As that trial progressed in Bolton, Marcus was outraged that Bandi's Indian barrister was trying to convince the jury to give his client a slap on the wrist for running the opium den since it wasn't actually illegal. The cockfighting and dog fighting were different. Those crimes and the deaths of all the addicts plus the theft of Chadwick's money persuaded the judge to impose a sentence of ten years in prison when a guilty verdict was returned.

All in all, Marcus was quite pleased with himself. He had kept his rank, unlike the Superintendent who'd been demoted and reassigned to the village of Westhoughton.

Marcus was still stuck with Walsh as his sidekick, but the young constable was coming along, though they weren't making much progress with the unexplained death at the local brewery.

Chapter 35

All's Well

Marcus was delighted and humbled to be asked to act as Deschanel's best man, though he got the feeling Foster Marsh's nose was out of joint because he hadn't been chosen.

"I owe my manager a lot," Edouard had replied when he'd mentioned it. "But my debt to you can never be repaid."

The wedding took place in the Bolton Registry Office. It was an informal affair with Maria Lonsdale and Angela Proctor acting as Maggie's attendants. The bride joked that she was probably the only woman who ever had a chorus line as her bridesmaids.

Even Emerson Dean came and his offer of congratulations seemed genuine.

Determined not to dwell overlong on his own lonely bachelor state, Marcus enjoyed the happy occasion.

Seeing the happiness of the newly-married couple at the wedding, Marcus was proud of the part he'd played in their lives, though, ironically, it was Fred Chadwick's incredible pride in his own debauchery that had provided the ultimate proof of Deschanel's innocence. Ken Swales was as much

Chadwick's victim as the poor girl who couldn't live with the shame of being raped.

Marcus wondered how many other men, or perhaps women, had thirsted to kill Fred Chadwick.

~

MAGGIE HAD SPENT her adult life playing a part on stage. As she and Edouard stood before the officiant in the Registry Office, she prayed for guidance as she took up her most important role. Loving, honoring, and obeying Edouard would be easy. Succeeding as the wife of a well-to-do businessman would be more difficult.

The tale of her determined efforts to prove Edouard innocent had spread throughout the county. Local folk celebrated her as a survivor, a woman with Lancashire grit. But Bolton's upper classes would have no respect for a music hall performer and even less for the former wife of Fred Chadwick.

She'd suggested quitting the music hall, but Edouard would have none of it. He insisted that people would come to change their opinions. Born and bred in Bolton, she knew more about local social prejudices than he did. Nevertheless, she resolved to improve the reputation of *The Hippodrome* and had already begun redecorating and refurbishing. Some of *Shangri-La's* patrons had started to trickle in to the performances.

People sometimes had to be turned away from the theater. If they didn't get there early enough, they were out of luck. The new comedian was proving to be very popular. Given Swales' conviction and his advent at the very moment the show had lost its comedian, there was a great deal of new speculation about the previous comedian's sudden death.

Lost in thought, Maggie suddenly realized the officiant was

eyeing her expectantly. "I do," she exclaimed, hoping that was the appropriate response.

Edouard's smile indicated it was and also reassured her she had no reason to fear for the future. He loved her and that's all that mattered. She'd survived a brutal marriage. She could surely shine in a happy one.

EDOUARD CONSIDERED himself the most fortunate of men. He was marrying a woman he loved to distraction. Maggie had already given notice and moved her personal belongings from the flat on Bank Street. The rag and bone man had been only too happy to load the decrepit furniture onto his wagon.

Shangri-La was busier and more profitable than ever. Rumor had it a few of his snootier customers had apparently sworn never to darken the store's door again, but he was confident they would eventually return. Maggie doubted his assertion that her occasional presence in the shop would give it a certain cachet, but he knew enough about selling to wealthy patrons to know he was right. The moneyed people in Bolton weren't the old aristocracy. They were mostly self-made men who harbored fewer prejudices.

Certainly, Maggie's presence in his apartment made it a warmer, more comfortable place. It now felt like home.

Marcus Halliwell cleared his throat, jolting him back to the present. "I do," he declared, earning a heart-stopping smile from his bride.

The rest of the short ceremony proceeded smoothly, he and Maggie making their solemn vows. They signed the register, then rode to *Shangri-La* in his carriage festooned with pompoms. His sleek little mare had always been a high-stepper, but, today, Cereste was clearly proud of the plume Albert had attached to her bridle.

A crowd of applauding clerks and customers greeted their entry into the main store. Maggie was magnificent as she greeted people graciously and thanked them. He didn't wish to be rude, but the desire to get his bride safely into the apartment took precedence over politeness. People would understand why a newly-married man was in a hurry to be alone with his new wife. He took Maggie's arm and escorted her quickly to their private domain.

Chapter 36

Burlesque

When they were finally alone in his apartment, Edouard flopped down on the settee, eased off his shoes and drew Maggie into his lap.

"You know, my love," Maggie crooned seductively, tracing a finger across his lips. "I'm trying to raise the tone of performances at *The Hippodrome.*"

"Yes," he answered cautiously, wondering where the conversation was headed.

"Did you also know that, at one time, Fred wanted to turn the theater into a burlesque show?"

There was something about the way his wife fluttered her eyelashes at him that gave Edouard a clue to her intentions. "I didn't know that. Was it you dissuaded him?"

"Oh, he never listened to me, but he knew I would have quit the show. I'd never take my clothes off for strangers, no matter how hard he tried to bully me."

A long silence followed during which Edouard's lascivious thoughts ran rampant. Was she waiting for him to ask? Finally, he had to speak. "Burlesque is quite popular in Paris, you know."

"I've heard that," she replied, slowly peeling off an elbow-length glove.

His cock reacted predictably when she slowly caressed his face with the glove. "Maggie," he rasped, groaning when she ground her bottom against his arousal. "You learn fast."

"You've turned me into a wanton," she whispered, cradling his face in her hands. "Would you like me to perform a striptease for you? After all, you're not a stranger."

"*Oui*," was all he could manage from his dry throat.

"It will be my wedding gift to you," she said as she rose from the settee and peeled off the other glove.

MAGGIE HOPED she could pull this off without making a complete fool of herself. Singing a few popular songs and telling jokes was one thing, striptease quite another.

Soon after her marriage to Fred, he'd begun to criticize everything about her body. She was too fat, or too thin. Her breasts were too small, or too big. As a result, she rarely undressed in front of him.

But Edouard made her feel desirable. He loved her curves. All she had to do was combine that certainty with her love of performing.

One look at the expectation in his green eyes was proof enough there was no turning back.

She slowly untied the ribbons of her bonnet, removed it and tossed it to Edouard.

"Bravo," he said with a smile.

The pins in her hair came next. As the chestnut tresses fell to her waist, his low growl gave her courage. She raised the hem of her skirts and kicked off the satin slippers she'd worn for the wedding. Putting one foot on the settee, she slid the garter down her leg. He put it to his nose when she tossed it to him.

As she peeled off her hose, his intense gaze gave her confidence. A seasoned performer could always tell when her audience was enjoying the show. The optimistic Maggie was back.

By the time she'd removed both garters and hose, he'd flared his nostrils and was restlessly shifting his weight on the settee.

Edouard resisted the urge to leap from the settee and tear off Maggie's clothes. She was enjoying performing for him. What else should he have expected from a darling of the music hall?

She even managed to make the removal of the ribbon around her neck seem erotic.

He already knew the bodice of the wedding gown from the House of Worth buttoned down the front. He'd eagerly anticipated unfastening it, but watching Maggie slowly undo each button turned his arousal to granite. Hooded eyes watched him. She knew full well the effect she was having on him and that only increased his desire.

Removal of the bodice revealed the top of a corset he recognized, as well as the chemise beneath. Her eyes widened seductively when he growled.

The flounce came next, then she wiggled herself out of the skirt. Turning her back to him, she stuck out her bottom provocatively as she unfastened the ties of the bustle then stepped out of the hooped underskirt.

He wasn't certain how he managed to sit still while she struggled out of the corset then lifted the chemise over her head and spread her arms wide.

He'd seen her generous breasts before, but as she stood before him clad only in pantalets, her body struck him as more tempting than ever. When she tucked her thumbs into the waist of the pantalets, he could wait no longer. "Magnificent performance," he declared as he scooped her up and carried her into the bedroom.

~

MAGGIE EXPECTED Edouard would want her to keep on the pantalets. He liked making love to her in the crotchless unmentionables. It came as a surprise when he deposited her on the bed, lifted her hips, and pulled off the pantalets.

"Now, Temptress," he growled. "You're going to lie there naked while I tease you the way you teased me."

The glint in his eyes promised excitement, but the bulge in his trousers made it doubtful he'd last much longer before entering her. Nevertheless, she'd enjoyed her performance and was gratified he had too.

Eyes narrowed, he shrugged off his morning coat then undid his cravat. Next, he peeled off his waistcoat.

When he embarked on the buttons of his shirt, she opened her legs. She resisted the urge to giggle when he fixed his gaze on her mons and his fingers fumbled with the buttons.

"*Méchante*," he rasped.

Trousers, drawers and hose were hurriedly removed in short order when she squeezed a nipple and licked her lips.

She'd seen Edouard naked before, but it suddenly struck her how lucky she was to be married to such a well-endowed man who was as concerned for her pleasure as much as for his own. "Come to me," she whispered, elated when he covered her with his warm body.

~

EDOUARD WAS ready to thrust inside his wife, but she was close to release and he couldn't deny himself that pleasure. She played with a nipple while he suckled the other, stoking his smug belief he'd helped her overcome some of her inhibitions.

Craving the sweet taste of her juices, he knelt between her bent legs and suckled her nubbin, grasping her thighs when she soared, breathlessly screaming his name.

They'd fulfilled a fantasy, one they'd perhaps both held secretly. Wanting to experience another on this magical evening, he lay flat on his back, flipped her on top and eased her down on his arousal.

She opened her eyes, stared into his, put her hands on his chest and smiled. Head thrust back, breasts pouting, she then proceeded to ride him to heaven, all the while playing with herself.

"Maggie," he yelled as his sperm bathed her womb and she cried out her fulfillment.

Historical Footnotes

COTTON COPS

You may be wondering why I gave this series the title COTTON COPS MYSTERIES. It's a play on the word for a spindle used in the cotton industry (cop) and, of course, the word for a policeman. http://revealinghistories.org.uk/why-was-cotton-so-important-in-north-west-england/objects/two-cotton-cops.html

BON MARCHE.

This famous store did exist in Paris. *Arcadia* and *Shangri-La* are figments of my imagination. https://en.wikipedia.org/wiki/Le_Bon_March%C3%A9

LANCASHIRE MUSIC HALL SONGS

https://www.gutenberg.org/cache/epub/55921/pg55921-images.html

OPIUM

Early in the nineteenth century, opium was legal in Britain and widely used in medicines such as laudanum. Many middle-class people used opium as a fashionable recreational drug, but working class folks often turned to the drug to deaden the harsh realities of life.

The recreational use of opium became popular in Britain in Victorian and Edwardian times. Opium dens were places where people could smoke opium in a social setting. They were established in many urban areas. British opium dens were described in Victorian novels as mysterious and dangerous places, fueling the public's imagination.

Opium dens were mainly found in London and other ports.

British opium dens catered to different social classes. Opium dens for the wealthy and elite offered luxurious surroundings and high-quality opium. Dens that catered to the working class provided a more basic setting and lower-quality opium. Although all classes were affected, the consequences for working-class people could be more severe. Addicted breadwinners could prioritize opium over their family's needs, spending a significant portion of their income on the drug.

Opium addiction became problematic in Britain, just as it was in China. Accidental overdoses were common, as was long-term dependency, often leading to chronic health problems.

BOLTON

I chose Bolton as the setting for this story and the others in the series for one simple reason—I was born and went to school there! https://en.wikipedia.org/wiki/Bolton

You may be aware that I'm an amateur genealogist. Many of my nineteenth-century ancestors worked as spinners in the cotton mills.

You'll find a good picture of the ancient pub, *Ye Old Man and Scythe* in the Wikipedia article.

LANCASHIRE

The Industrial Revolution changed Lancashire forever. Its damp climate was ideal for the cotton industry which developed rapidly. Fortunes were made by the *nouveau riche* industrialists. These self-made men became the new "aristocracy", their power based on wealth and not titles and privilege.

Roger Sandiford, the hero of *The Heart's Choice*, is one such mill owner.

Lancashire was the first industrial society in the world, the place where anything and everything was made and where coal was mined. It was the birthplace of the factory system and it needed a big population to operate the mines and factories. The first canal in the world was built in Lancashire, with more canals and railways following by the early 1830's. The workforce required was far bigger than the existing Lancashire population and had to be imported from other counties, and from Ireland and Scotland. These men and women came from rural areas to live crammed together in the cities. Villages fast became towns.

Statistics show that Lancashire had a considerable crime rate compared with the rest of the country. In 1836, 2568 Lancastrians were convicted or tried for serious offenses.

Some towns formed their own police forces but there was a growing demand for a county-wide force modeled on the London Metropolitan Police, brought into existence in 1829 by Sir Robert Peel. https://en.wikipedia.org/wiki/Robert_Peel

The Lancashire Constabulary was formed in 1840. https://en.wikipedia.org/wiki/Lancashire_Constabulary

THE COTTON FAMINE

https://en.wikipedia.org/wiki/Lancashire_Cotton_Famine

TONGE CEMETERY

Tonge Cemetery was the first municipal cemetery in Bolton

when it opened on New Year's Eve 1856 and was known simply as Bolton cemetery.

In 2002 the English Heritage organization considered Tonge Cemetery to be of sufficient historical interest to be placed on the Register of Parks and Gardens as a Grade II listed site.

Heaton Cemetery is now the busiest cemetery in Bolton with around 250 interments per annum. The cemetery also contains dedicated areas for both religions and communities, these include Ukrainian, Polish, Latvian, Russian, Muslim and Hindu.

Personal note: Many of my ancestors are buried in Heaton Cemetery.

QUADRICYCLE

https://www.alamy.com/an-engraving-depicting-a-quadricy cle-with-room-for-two-persons-to-sit-side-by-side-its-width-made-it-an-inconvenient-vehicle-dated-19th-century-image235220770.html

BOLTON BOROUGH POLICE

https://en.wikipedia.org/wiki/Bolton_Borough_Police
BTW, my father was present at the disaster mentioned in the article.

POLICING IN THE 19TH CENTURY & POLICE VIOLENCE

https://www.amazon.com/Victorian-Policing-Gaynor-Haliday/dp/1526706121

STILLETT'S

https://sillettsfunerals.co.uk/
Actually established in 1875, a few years after our story.

EAST INDIANS IN ENGLAND

https://en.wikipedia.org/wiki/British_Indians

CARRERAS (Black Cat Cigarettes)

https://lookup.london/carreras-cigarette-factory/

THREE LITTLE PIXIES

We know this fable as *The Three Little Pigs*, but the original story revolved around three little pixies.

BLACKROD

https://en.wikipedia.org/wiki/Blackrod

THE ENGLISH WORKING CLASS

https://www.amazon.com/Making-English-Working-Penguin-Classics-ebook/dp/B002RI9W8

About Anna

As an amateur genealogist (aka an addict of family tree research) I became obsessed with tracing my English roots back to the Norman Conquest in the 11th century. This turned out to be a pipe dream since I am not descended from the nobility and records were not kept for "common folks" until much later. Even then, early parish records are often indecipherable.

As a result, I began to write stories about a noble medieval family I conjured from my imagination. The Montbryces were born.

Like many people, I had an inner compulsion to write one good book. What was originally intended as that one book about my fictional family eventually became the 12-book series, The Montbryce Legacy.

In other words, writing superseded genealogy as my principal addiction, and I have since published more than 60 novels and novellas. Almost all are historical romances that feature Vikings, Highlanders, medieval knights, Elizabethan goldsmiths or Regency aristocrats. You can find more details on my website https://annamarkland.com/.

I've lived most of my life in Canada, though I was born in the UK. An English grammar school education instilled in me a love of European history which continues to this day. While I may boast of being a proud Canadian, I'm still a Lancashire lass at heart.

Before becoming a full-time writer, I was an elementary

school teacher, a job I loved. I then worked as administrator for a world-wide disaster relief organization.

I love cats, although I haven't been able to bring myself to adopt another one since unexpectedly losing Topaz a few years ago.

I have few domestic skills. You'll notice most of my heroines hate sewing!

I try to follow three simple writing guidelines. I give my characters free rein to tell their story, which often turns out to be different from the original version in my head. I'm a firm believer in love at first sight. My protagonists may initially deny the attraction but, eventually, my heroes and heroines find their soul mates. It seems only natural then to include scenes of intimacy enjoyed by people who love each other deeply. I believe such intimacy is wholesome. Historical accuracy is important to me, although I have been known to tweak history when necessary. I write romance because I find happy endings very satisfying.

You can find me on all the usual social media platforms. On Facebook as Anna Markland and Anna Markland Novels, on Instagram as annamarkland, on Twitter as @annamarkland, and Pinterest and BookBub as Anna Markland. I also have a reader group on Facebook called Markland's Merrymakers and new members are always welcome.

I acknowledge the invaluable assistance of my beta reader extraordinaire, Maria McIntyre, my editor, Sue-Ellen Welfonder, and my PA, Alison Pridie.

Also by Anna Markland

Cotton Cops Mystery Series

The Heart's Choice

Music Hall Queen

OTHER SERIES

Montbryce Legacy

Earls are Wild

FitzRam Family Dynasty

Clash of the Tartans

Montbryce Dynasty

The House of Pendray

Viking Roots Medieval

Von Wolfenberg Dynasty

The Caledonia Chronicles

Highland Whisky Kings

The UnDukes

Ruff Wooing

About the Author

Anna is a USA Today bestseller who has authored more than sixty award-winning and much-loved Medieval, Victorian, Viking, Highlander, Elizabethan and Regency historical romances. No matter the historical or geographic setting, many of her series recount the adventures of successive generations of one family, with emphasis on the importance of ancestry and honor. A detailed list with links can be found at https://www.annamarkland.com/

Getting the word out about her book is vital to its success. If you enjoy this book, please consider writing a review. Reviews help other readers find books.

* 9 7 8 1 6 4 8 3 9 9 6 8 8 *